THE
MESSAGE

Agents of Cosmic Intelligence
An Alternate View of History

BILL HARVEY

The Human Effectiveness Institute
Gardiner, New York

Published in 2022 by
The Human Effectiveness Institute

ISBN: 978-0-918538-17-8 Trade Paperback
978-0-918538-18-5 eBook

Library of Congress Control Number: 2022919911

For information write to:
The Human Effectiveness Institute
12 Amani Drive, Gardiner, NY 12525
HumanEffectivenessInstitute.org

Editing, book design and typesetting by Yana Lambert
Cover art by Bruce Rolff / RolffImages.com/
Cover design by Yana Lambert & Christine K. Niver

Printed in the United States of America on FSC-certified paper for F. Scott Fitzgerald

1

Martin Williams' father was a career soldier, like his grandfather and his great grandfather, and the men in his family they talked about from long before his time. So, it was natural for him to assume that he too was going to be a soldier. But something about it bothered him from his earliest memories. As he grew older, he'd go back and ponder the source of these doubts—doubts he never expressed openly. Eventually he concluded that some very deep part of him, intrinsic to his being, felt that the job he had to do was even larger than fighting to protect free people. But that deep part of him never revealed what that big job was. He waited and hoped that someday he would understand himself at least that much, meanwhile setting about on a military career.

His parents once took him to a museum when he was very young. It was one of his earliest memories. The museum was hosting an exhibition on Venus Aphrodite, replete with statues and paintings of her throughout the ages. He imagined he knew Venus long ago, though he had no idea what that meant. When he reached puberty, he began to dream of making love with Venus. When he began dating, he picked the girls who looked like the Venus of his dreams, blonde, colorfully made up, a graceful neck, inviting, mischievously yet innocently flaunting her lush body.

Growing up, Martin noticed how often he made mistakes of one kind or another, which led him to become introspective and very observant of his own behavior, internally as well as externally. He told himself that mistakes could turn his whole life into a waste. He saw that before he acted, a flurry of conflicting impulses in his mind would present a range of possible actions, then he would *apparently choose one path and take it*. The word "apparently" appeared in his mind often, because he was well aware that reality could differ from appearances. He had become an avid reader of books on science, and science fiction novels from the age of five. He became an agnostic the more he felt drawn to science. (Nevertheless, one Christmas he was touched by the meaning of the holiday and sang baby Jesus to sleep in his mind.) To him, science meant certainty, and the avoidance of surety until the evidence was inescapable. So, he regarded whatever he thought in his mind with a grain of salt.

He noticed that right before he took any particular action, the voices or thoughts in his head intimating which action he should take could be identified as the internalized voices of his father and mother. He formed an impression of the advice each one would give him, and became given to predicting how they would advise him in whatever the current situation happened to be. He kept track of the outcomes and could tell that sometimes the advice of either parent could lead him to take an action that was regrettable. One time in self-defense he really hurt a boy more than necessary, which had been sanctioned by his mind's predicted father's advice. Another time he was so civilized with his young friends that they embarrassed him about it, his behavior having been advocated by his mind's predicted mother's advice. By the time he was ten years old, he realized he had an advisor in his mind whose track record was flawless in giving action recommendations that satisfied him in retrospect. Often that "voice" didn't even use words—it was more like a hunch he understood without having used words to explain it to himself. By age twelve, he had figured out something strange was going on. He had many, many hunches each day, and they always turned out to be right. He also noticed that his mind made up things *like* hunches, which almost always gave bad advice. He very gradually learned to tell the difference between his real intuitions and the mock intuitions that apparently some part of his mind made up to make itself feel smart.

Once, at around age twelve, the point of view in his mind that gave him the real hunches used words for a change—words accompanied by a strong feeling of realizing a deep truth. The words were, "I am God... and so is everybody else." That felt truly weird because he was agnostic, and totally committed to science. He tried to figure out what those words meant, and why it felt so true—like it had to be true for some scientific reason that his mind could not yet explain to him. For the rest of his life, he would work to unravel this mystery.

Ω

Captain Martin Williams, rangy and sandy-haired, was being briefed by his superior officer in a dark cave in Afghanistan. Both men used small flashlights to illuminate the map. The Major pointed to a rocky pass. "Intel says take your men through here."

Martin had a hunch. He pointed at the next pass to the west. "What about this one?" he asked.

"Why that one?"

"Just a hunch."

The Major looked exasperated. "Marty, don't start that crap."

Martin shrugged.

He gathered and moved his men relatively soundlessly through the moonless night. As they approached the pass they had been ordered to take, Martin, leading the way, held up his hand and the company halted. He picked a fireteam and pointed up to the ridge on the left. "Make a deep recon just the other side of the ridge line. If you meet resistance, dig in and protect our flank, then scramble down and rejoin us," he ordered. "No radios unless there's a firefight." All their helmets had radios. The enemy had learned how to listen in, however. The enemy was a branch of ISIL that had recently taken over the country by crushing the Taliban.

The rest of the company was surprised to be waiting in place as the four soldiers disappeared into the night. Martin kept them waiting five minutes. They heard and saw a firefight erupt just over the ridge to the west. Martin motioned his men forward at a fast trot. The 140 men ran through the pass. Noting craters in the ground, Martin figured out that the unit his fireteam had engaged had been working on zeroing in mortars on the pass they were running through, and he sprinted forward at the fastest speed he could manage. His men took the hint.

Ω

His superior apologized. "Good work, Marty. You'd have lost fewer men if I'd listened to your hunch."

"Sir, I have a hunch you should check the source of the intel," Martin said, and his boss nodded sensibly.

Ω

"Sir, you want to give me my own command because of my hunches?" Martin laughed out loud. Was he dreaming? This was ridiculous. Wearing dress uniform as ordered, he was meeting with a bunch of Generals in the Pentagon.

"This comes straight from the top. The president has given top secret orders. Intel confirms the existence of a psychic unit within the Russian army. We've got to have our own, and we've got a lot of catching up to do. We've got to assign it to somebody who we can trust, one of our own, not some civilian, although you are free to recruit civilians to work under your command. This is a mental arms race. The president feels that it could be the most important arms race we're in," a five-star said. "He wants this Theta Force to report to him personally."

Martin checked in with himself, and found that this made him very excited and happy. But he had a hunch.

"Sir, may I speak plainly?" Martin asked, looking around although addressing the five- star, who was senior in the room. The general grunted and others nodded. "Sir, I could cock this up. I can train people to use their minds the way I do, I'll need help finding people who have the raw talents both within and beyond the Army, and I can use my hunches to help protect Theta. What I can't do while doing all that is to handle the politics of running a command that reports so high."

"What are you asking for?" the five-star queried.

"I would like to be the executive officer of Theta, in charge of training and security. I don't want to be the commanding officer. I'm not ready."

The group looked at each other. They had all, including Williams, graduated from West Point, where they had been trained to want to move up the ladder as fast as possible. *This guy is weird, maybe he's right to say he isn't ready for command of what is probably going to be a battalion-size unit.*

"Anyone in mind?" the five-star asked.

Williams nodded. He had done his homework. "Colonel Tim Shannon," he said. He had observed Shannon, who commanded the brigade of elite troops from all branches of service in which Williams had been just a cog. Shannon always got nearly all of his people out. Williams had a hunch that Shannon could also be trained to have hunches, and he was glad nobody asked him to explain this particular hunch, which had come to him in a dream. In the dream—set in a brightly lit place, almost too bright to see, with beautiful white ornate temples everywhere—Martin was a teacher, and Shannon was his star pupil, wearing the same bushy mustache that Shannon now sported.

The five-star looked around. Shannon's current boss looked irritated, but in the spirit of cooperation, allowed reluctantly, "We can make do without him in Afghanistan."

"One more request, please, sir?" Martin boldly surprised them all. He could hear the common thought in the room: *cheeky.* The senior officer nodded cautiously.

"Please don't ever tell Colonel Shannon that you offered me his command," Martin enjoined, and they all signaled agreement.

$$\Omega$$

Seana Moon's earliest memory was of being in a baby seat in the back of a car. Her parents, whom she loved above all else, were in the front, laughing and talking to each other. Her heart was full of happiness and everything was perfect in her life, being off on some adventure with her parents. She suddenly sensed something bad and began shrieking a wordless warning a moment before a bullet came through the driver's side windshield.

As she grew older, she always sought out more information about the tragedy in which her parents both perished, her father killed by the bullet and her mother killed in the crash. The authorities could only surmise that it was the kind of test gangs used to decide whether to take in a newcomer.

Seana's perfect life disappeared in an instant. First there was the horrible sound of things smashing and the unforgettably awful sounds her parents made as they died. Then the smell and smoke that made her cough and unable to breathe, none of which mattered because she only wanted to go wherever they were going. She was surrounded by frantic strangers, who manhandled her in their panic to free her from the car, and then the memories blurred as she was taken from place to place, examined, talked about as if she wasn't there. Then some nice person would try to comfort her but she was inconsolable, crying all the time, crying herself to sleep, crying herself awake, realizing that she would never see her Mummy and Daddy again—though some part of her somehow doubted that.

When the tears finally subsided and she was able to think about what had happened, though still just a toddler, Seana had the strange idea that she herself had been the target. *Where did that terrible idea come from?* Wherever it came from, it made her hate herself. She forced herself to give up that idea and convinced herself it had not been her fault. She took this precocious act of will before she learned to talk, never realizing how unusual that was.

Seana was taken in and brought up by her Aunt Anna and Uncle Jim. Anna made her living as a professional psychic. Jim was a car salesman and though not psychic he had seen enough to convince him that Anna's talents were real. Anna worked for wealthy people, reading tarot cards for them, and advising them accordingly. On occasion the police also called her in for help on an unsolved case.

Seana thought she saw lights in the air around Anna sometimes, and when she took a picture of Anna with her first cell phone, the photo picked up the lights around Anna's head.

Anna explained that the lights were her protectors. She pointed to one of the lights. "This is Jocko," she said. "Jocko is very big and carries a long, pointed weapon."

"A spear?" Seana asked.

"No, a directed-energy weapon," Anna disclosed.

All her young life, Seana was open to the existence of "magic"—as she thought of it—in all its forms. Nothing was impossible if you didn't rule it out in your mind, Anna had taught her. Anna taught in many ways, often dressing up the three of them (with Jim) in costumes and carrying out strange rituals. She demonstrated the use of the I Ching, Ouija board and the pendulum. She guided Seana through concentration, contemplation, and meditation exercises. She taught her how to read tarot cards, and Seana started to give readings for money so she could go to college without saddling herself with debt.

In college Seana studied philosophy and psychology. Her friends at school partied with psychedelics, from mescaline, psilocybin, and Molly, to LSD, 25i-NBOMe, and ayahuasca. Seana tried them all but always left the party early and went off alone when tripping, to do serious self-investigation and to pray for contact with God. She had no set religion but had always sensed the presence of an intelligence far greater than human.

Ω

When Tim Shannon was given command of Theta and introduced to Martin Williams as his second-in-command, the two hit it off from the start. Tim knew of Martin as one of his Company commanders, and when being briefed about plans for Theta, he was told that Williams was the only blooded combat officer in the U.S. Army who had shown any promise of having psychic abilities. Martin had learned to have great respect for Shannon, having observed him make the right strategic decisions in tough combat situations, and having seen how fraternally and protectively he treated all the men and women under his command.

Martin felt that if reincarnation happened to be true, Shannon might have long ago been his star pupil, just like in the dream.

In the early days of Theta, the two spent their time training Tim to not block his innate psychic powers, which Martin now claimed that everyone has, causing Tim to regard some of Martin's ideas with a modicum of skepticism. But there was no denying the effects: Tim soon found that he could tell his own real hunches from wishful thinking, and was amazed at the accuracy of true hunches. He also started to be able to read thoughts that Martin communicated to him.

Shannon started to recruit people and bring them into Theta, some from the U.S. armed services and some who were civilians, all now given officer status in the U.S. Army. American intelligence agencies and law enforcement agencies, whose top officials had received secret orders from the president to aid in the hunt for America's psychics, tested thousands of claimed or suspected psychics, finding only a small percentage able to pass the usual tests such as the Rhine cards. Those who made the cut were presented to Tim, who then made his own assessment and decided which people to take, largely based on his own hunches.

Theta had offices in the Pentagon but its main base hid in plain view in a suburban neighborhood in Virginia. It had been

a Howard Johnson motel a long time ago. Now it masquer-
aded as a no-name motel that was mysteriously always sold
out. Within a few months the base housed more than a hundred recruits along with Tim and Martin.

Seana was one of the first recruits. More than one intelligence agency knew that she made her living as a psychic and
her clients included some of the wealthiest people in New York
City. Tim was surprised by her beauty, intelligence, and upbeat
nature. *This is the one woman in the world made just for me,*
he thought at first blush. He didn't take the thought seriously
at the time; their professional relationship strongly discour-
aged his paying any attention to that line of thought—besides
which she was just barely an adult at twenty-one, and he was
thirty-seven. Still, he found it extremely easy to talk to her and
when he asked her to read his mind she did so with amazing
accuracy.

"You are attracted to me, but that line of thinking is forbidden to you," she said without embarrassment.

Now getting used to being an Army officer, she addressed
him with decorum. "Sir, I can attest that I'm not the one woman
in the world that was made just for you. You're a gallant hero to
millions of women who watched you winning a war on television. I'm sure more than one of them would like to meet you."

They shared an easy laugh. *It might always have to be pla-
tonic,* he thought, but he loved her already. He gave himself
permission to love her as long as he didn't express his feelings
in any way. He hoped she was not reading his mind right now.

"Incidentally," he shared, "Martin and I agreed at the start
of Theta that among ourselves, we would not read each other's
minds except by invitation and in any emergencies."

Seana concurred, adding, "That's what all true psychics
believe too." She had met quite a few.

Tim drove them from the Pentagon to Theta's base outside
Arlington to meet Martin. When they arrived at the base, Tim
inquired and was told that Martin could be found in the hot
tub by the pool. The sun was just going down. Tim and Seana

dropped off their things in their respective rooms, put on their bathing suits and joined him.

Minutes later, watching from the hot tub and sipping vodka tonic from a plastic cup, Martin was galvanized seeing the two of them approach. He got it that Tim was bringing in a recruit to meet him. His mind immediately compared Seana to Venus and decided that this was not the real Venus coming back to him from his dreams or his imagination. Seana was petite whereas Venus was Junoesque. They both had wonderful curves and playful expressions, but Venus in his dreams was flirtatious while Seana projected a demure vulnerability. As she came closer, he could see that Seana had larger eyes and higher cheekbones. They were different women, though he quite appreciated Seana's appearance.

Ω

Templegard's body was sleeping in a cave in Afghanistan with his finger on a trigger. His consciousness was off in an enjoyable dream. In the dream he was on a cleaner mission in a spaceship with his comrades in arms. He recognized two of them easily, one being his former boss, Colonel Shannon, who had left the theater recently on a classified mission. Templegard was happy to see them back together.

The second one, a woman with black hair and pillowy lips, he recognized as the woman in half his dreams, so no surprise there. As always, she was alluring to him. Now she was dressed in some kind of tight-fitting black coverall. He liked the way it fit her. She smiled impishly at him.

Another woman he didn't recognize reminded him of somebody he must have once known. She was a curvy blonde with high cheekbones. He liked her right away.

And there was a man who seemed to be the leader. Templegard had never seen him before but he looked familiar somehow. Sandy hair, tall and muscular, eyes that took in everything.

They were all looking out through the huge transparent nose of the spaceship. From above the plane of the ecliptic

near Saturn, Templegard saw the ringed planet below forming a sort of line with Jupiter and Earth. He had a clear sense
this was as prophesied: his partners down on Earth, who had
forgotten their identities, were about to be jarred by a miracle.
Templegard sent them a prayer. Then he wondered who and
what he had been thinking about. After all, his partners were
right here on the ship.

Ω

Just east of New York City in a brick professional building,
most of his partners—who other than Shannon did not know
he existed, and didn't know who they really were themselves
either—were additionally unaware of the major events, mandated high in the multiverse governance, which were about to
befall them.

As if all that ignorance were not enough, they had plenty of
trouble already.

In the conference room with the large mirror on one wall,
Lieutenant Colonel Martin Williams held up Rhine cards only
he could see, and Major Jason Page tried to psychically detect
the symbol on each card held up.

Behind the one-way mirror in the next room, their boss,
Brigadier General Tim Shannon, sat with Congressman War-
ren Baynes, hearing the piped-in voices of Williams and Page,
and able to see the cards over Williams' shoulder. Page was
getting almost nothing right. Baynes' bejowled face radiated
disgust as he mumbled to himself. Shannon maintained an
impassive exterior while noting his political stock value drop-
ping by the second.

Williams said sympathetically to Jason, "Something distracted you during meditation."

"What was that?" Jason asked.

"Probably worrying about your score," Williams said and
smiled. Neither of them looked at the one-way mirror but they
knew they were both thinking of the source of pressure.

Shannon tapped the Bluetooth in his ear and said, "Try
the other one." Williams flinched at the word "try", looking let

down. *Sorry... I mean run the other one,* Shannon said telepathically to Williams, hoping the other would get his message. *Williams is better than the rest of them at ESP, so maybe he will,* Shannon thought.

Williams' smile returned.

Shannon signaled Baynes to turn his chair to face another one-way mirror in the room. As they rolled their swivel chairs in that direction, the lights came on in the exercise room. Jason had shed his outer clothes as he entered the room and flipped on the lights. Behind him came Lieutenant Colonel Ahmed Khan, wearing judo *gi*, followed by Williams and a pretty young woman, Seana Moon. Williams and Seana tied blindfolds over the eyes of Jason and Khan, adding high-tech "earmuffs" to block out all sound. Baynes peered hopefully at the proceedings through the one-way glass while Shannon maintained his poker face.

Stripped to the waist and barefoot, wearing only his U.S. Army fatigue pants, Jason looked like a young Black Adonis, exuding confidence. Khan looked much older and comparatively out of shape, although he obviously worked out daily.

"This fight seems kind of unequal," Baynes commented to Shannon in their dark observation room.

"Khan has been practicing blindfold fighting since he was four," Shannon disclosed.

Khan and Page began to circle. Page attacked Khan with a surprisingly well-aimed flying kick, Khan deflected it, Page rolled to his feet and continued circling.

"Wow!" Baynes said. Shannon looked grimly satisfied.

Baynes watched more attentively now. Page attacked Khan with a flying leg trip and they both went down, scuffled briefly, and came up circling.

"Why didn't you show me this first?" Baynes asked.

"That's the problem," Shannon replied. "You never know what's going to work, when."

"Sounds like all our other advanced weapons systems," Baynes muttered.

"Yeah. But we're finding out the things that block psychic power. We're going to discover all the blocks and learn how to keep them out of the way, someday—"

"Maybe someday—*if* you can show some results soon, so we can get this program put back in the budget—" Baynes dropped the other shoe.

"Put back?" Shannon felt the bottom fall out as Baynes nodded somberly. "Why didn't you tell me?"

"Why do you think I came to see you here in New York?"

Shannon turned from him and stared through the one-way mirror, bringing his sudden anger and angst under control. Page and Khan were exchanging a volley of Kung Fu attacks and parries.

"Williams sensed this coming..." Shannon mused. "You don't know how complicated... Seana is going to turn her head and look at me."

Baynes turned to watch Seana, thinking to himself how pretty he found her. She turned to look at the one-way mirror to where she knew Shannon was sitting, then turned back to her tablet, which showed the brainwaves of Jason and Khan.

"I knew I could make her do it just then," Shannon said. "If I'd waited a second, the confidence would have gone, and I couldn't have done it."

Baynes looked interested.

"Page is looking pretty good, huh?" Shannon went on, and Baynes nodded. "He's still embarrassed from the card test, trying to redeem himself," Shannon continued. "Think I can make him fail in there?"

Baynes shrugged.

"We've got to know how to make enemy psychics fail, you know, Mr. Baynes. You don't put our budget back in, this country is wide open to enemy psychics."

"It's not just up to me," Baynes objected.

"Watch this," Shannon said, reaching for the stars as he flicked his Bluetooth. "Seana, don't turn your head. Encourage Page—*don't* turn your head!"

Seana looked confused. Page at that moment body-blocked Khan, knocking the wind out of him. Khan recovered and they began to circle again.

"Hey, not bad, Jase!" Seana said. Page stopped, grinned, and started circling again.

"Can the side comments," Williams admonished her.

"Williams heard you order her to do it—" Baynes started questioningly.

"He doesn't want Page to guess that," Shannon explained.

Page made a series of attacks on Khan, who fell back fending them all off, until one of his defenses unintentionally hit Page on the chin. Jason went down clutching his jaw in pain. Khan ripped off his blindfold and he, Williams and Seana reflexively went to Page's side. Page got up, took off his blindfold, and rubbed his jaw, looking suspiciously at Seana and sheepish at the same time.

Baynes eyed his watch. "You have someone to take me to LaGuardia, Colonel?" he asked, hoping it would be Seana.

"I'll take you," Shannon said, sensing Baynes' interest in Seana and sparing her Baynes' lechery.

In the car, Shannon asked, "How much time do I have to come up with results I can show you?"

"I don't know," Baynes admitted. "What I also don't know is why the hell you're in New York. I'd think you'd be able to demonstrate results faster by keeping all Theta personnel together in your very expensively equipped main base in Virginia—"

"That was our recommendation too," Shannon surprised him by saying.

"So why are you in New York?"

"Orders."

"I know," Baynes said caustically. "Orders from the president. Secret orders." He suddenly turned to Shannon. "Did you vote for him?"

Shannon flicked a glance at him, answering, "No."

Baynes slapped his thigh. "I haven't found anybody that will admit having voted for him."

"We've had a lot of presidents like that," Shannon said calmly.

"We used to have great men—historic giants," Baynes said reprovingly and passionately. Shannon glanced at him again and decided the man was deeper than he had realized.

Baynes muttered as if to himself, "The prerogative of the Executive Branch. For all I know he could be using you to spy on his political enemies and covering it with a blanket of 'national security'." He looked at Shannon. "You know you wouldn't have gotten your original funding if it wasn't for me. Now I don't even know what you're working on."

This was a bluff on Baynes' part. The president wanted Theta, and it was the president's influence that made Theta happen, not Baynes', but almost no one knew that. Williams had been sworn to secrecy on that very point.

"I said we couldn't do fieldwork and demonstrate results at the same time—"

"Why New York," Baynes pressed. "You want me to roll pork barrels with you, son, you roll pork barrels with me. Why New York?"

Shannon owed this guy. Theta couldn't afford to lose him as their champion in Congress. He'd have to break a rule, which meant Baynes would have something on him. He had to trust Baynes. What a dumb thing to do. He did it anyway.

"That's where... the subject is."

"What subject?"

"The subject of surveillance."

"Who is he?"

"Can't... I've told you too much already."

"What's his importance?"

"He's demonstrated... some unusual effects... he could be a very powerful psychic."

"What are you going to do, recruit him?"

"Maybe... we don't know where his loyalties lie... he's a citizen now but wasn't born here..."

"All of the top Theta people had to be sent to New York to observe one guy you *might* recruit? What does he do, part the Red Sea?"

"Mr. Congressman, you're a pretty good agent yourself. I'll get you your results."

It is permanent night in the nuclear-proof main base of the Russian psychic force called Psychotronic Division One. It's a bustling underground city peopled by men and women clad in military-cut leatherlike black coveralls. There are brainwave, fMRI, and PET scanner laboratories, offices, weapons rooms, communications center, meeting hall and meeting rooms, dining area, a pool and gymnasium, and of course the barracks section.

In one particular room in the female officers' quarters, on one of the two beds, on top of the covers in a nightshirt, lay Nastassia Slayevsky, a stunning dark-haired fifteen-year-old girl of Chinese-Russian-Cuban descent, who happened to be one of Psychotronics' most promising new psychics in training. She lied back and closed her eyes, focusing on her breath going in and out.

She didn't really like working for Psychotronics. Inside she knew that her psychic gifts were reflections of her deep spiritual nature. Yet talk of anything spiritual was strictly forbidden in Psycho, as everyone called the unit. She had to live a lie every day because they had her parents in custody to coerce her cooperation.

And now, she was having these erotic sensations she had never experienced before.

She had orgasms in her sleep, while dreaming of the same man over and over. They had apparently spent many lives together, and she felt sure she would find him again in this lifetime.

Nastassia's erotic dreams had come to the attention of her roommate, who was a few years older than her and very understanding. Yet it was still embarrassing, so she sought to sublimate her libido into daydreams instead. Having a powerful imagination, her daydreams felt almost as good as the real thing.

She daydreamed about her dream man, and then one of the guards caught her eye and she started splitting her daydreams to include the guard, whose very common name was Ivan.

As she lay focusing on her breath, in a few moments the fog cleared in her inner vision and she could see a dark smoky room in which soldiers were playing cards and drinking vodka. She could see Ivan's rugged now stubbly face.

Ivan, she called out to him, and she could see that he had heard. He had in fact seen her eyes. *Ivan, I need you.* He tossed in his cards and stood up abruptly. The other soldiers laughed sympathetically as he had lost some money.

Soon he silently slid into her room. This had happened before. He hoped this would be the time she would go all the way. Ivan whispered, "Were you really calling me—?"

Nastassia signaled him to be silent and to come closer. He approached unsurely. She reached up and pulled his head down to whisper into her ear.

"Sergeant," she whispered.

He tried to stand up but she restrained him with surprising strength.

"Lieutenant? Can I bring you something?" he whispered, afraid to cross the line with an officer, but sorely tempted to try.

"I saw you looking at me today," she whispered.

He looked at her, trying to figure her out, then moved to kiss her. She coyly avoided the kiss.

"Sergeant," she whispered again. He tried straightening up again but she still restrained him.

"I need..." He looked at her, barely daring to hope. "My feet are killing me..."

As she released him, he reluctantly moved to the foot of the bed and began to massage her feet.

"Oh, yes..." she whispered, making occasional hushed moans. In her imagination this was just the prelude so she was able to enjoy sex without having it, and she assumed he was doing the same. She was correct.

Ω

Williams and Seana had left the Theta offices soon after Shannon and Baynes departed, taking the elevator upstairs to his room. Her room hadn't been used since they got to New York. Recently the two had realized that they knew each other from earlier lives. They didn't remember what their relationship had been except that it had been friendly and close. They tried it on for size as lovers, which was convenient as they both had libidos and no time off. Still, neither felt sure that they were destined to be lovers forever. This transparency with each other created an ambiguity both just lived with for the time being.

First, they made love standing up in the shower and then dried off a bit and laid towels over the bedspread; he sat cross-legged on the bed and she straddled him. As she had taught him (although it somehow seemed familiar), this was called the Yab-yum position in Tantric yoga. They looked into each other's eyes and did not move. They each began to touch the other ever so lightly. He felt how soft, warm, and taut her skin was. She felt how muscular and hairy he was, and yet how gentle and caring. They had become the best of friends. She idolized him, and he adored her. Though their relationship seemed more mental than passionate, it made them both happy.

Later they dined in the room. After the waiter had come back and cleared the room, they got into bed and cuddled. He could see that something was bothering her. He kissed her ear.

"Worrying, are you?" he asked her.

"No," she replied, "I can get along without Theta—they close it down, I go back to reading tarot cards for a living. Maybe I'd even pursue an advanced degree in psychology and see where that leads."

"We have other even better options, you know," Williams gently pleaded.

"We? You wouldn't leave the Army."

"Perhaps. But I wouldn't let you go."

"Marty, the Army's your whole life."

"Now *you* are," he said, suddenly realizing it was true.

Ω

Williams and Seana were in Tim's office at the close of the business day. Seana, dressed in low-cut low-back clubwear, was just about to leave.

"You look great," Shannon said admiringly, recalling how taken he'd been with Seana when they first met. He'd played it cool for too long, however, and she and Marty had come together first. He regretted his cautious inaction more than he let show.

"I don't feel great about this," Seana said levelly, "I warned you it's a waste of time. Now it's putting us out of business. Why do I still have to go through with it?"

"Orders," Shannon said simply.

"Orders, yeah—orders. You Army guys love that word," she said, and went on her way.

Ω

In the back of a helicopter, his exhausted body exfiltrated, Templegard dreamed he was back with the team on the spaceship, happy to see them all. Through the transparent dome, they could now see that Earth, Jupiter, Saturn, and Uranus were nearly in a perfect line. Again, Templegard sensed something big was about to happen, something rare.

Ω

Seana took a robot taxi from Penn Station and arrived late at the upper Park Avenue address. The doorman came to help her out of the cab, admiring her legs then looking proper as he straightened up to help her over the curb. He of course wore a sidearm—all doormen in New York City did nowadays. His backup stood just inside the lobby, with an automatic rifle. The better buildings all had security backups.

"You must be Ms. Moon," he said. "Please go right up to the penthouse. Mr. Mann's private elevator is the one all the way on the right." He pointed, then turned to open the door of the next arriving car.

"Thanks." She shot friendly glances to all the security cameras she could spot as she crossed the lobby, then smiled sweetly at the one she could see in the elevator. A Hieronymus Bosch painting full of weird creatures hung in the elevator, covered with armored glass, and very securely fastened to the elevator wall.

She stepped off the elevator right into the fabulous suite and could appreciate the skyline in two directions. The butler greeted her.

"Good evening, Miss."

"Good evening, Chumley," she said, and left him to wonder how she knew his name and its correct pronunciation.

"Ah yes, Miss, I recall we were introduced at the party Mrs. McKenzie gave. Mr. Mann is waiting for you in the exercise room... right this way, Miss."

He led her past spectacular art and statuary into the exercise room, outfitted with padded floors and floor-to-ceiling mirrored walls—and one wall of windows looking out at Manhattan. Nautilus equipment sat in one corner and free weights in another. Ari Mann, a handsome young man with a wiry, muscular body—showing it off by wearing only scant black underwear—sparred with his trainer Doctor Chi, dressed in judo *gi*.

Exuding a manic energy, Ari reacted to her entry by stepping up his attack. A flurry of attacks and counterattacks culminated in Ari knocking Chi to the mat with a rather cruel blow. Chi leapt to his feet, apparently unharmed, bowed, and smilingly applauded his student and boss. Mann bowed to him briefly and stepped to Seana, moving to kiss her on the mouth. She turned her head slightly and took his kiss on the cheek.

"Delightful to see you again," Ari said in his Israeli-Russian accent. He had been born in Russia and lived in Israel before coming to the United States.

"Same here."

"Dr. Chi, Seana Moon," Ari introduced them. Chi bowed.

"Pleasure," Seana said.

Mann looked down at himself and up at her. "My apologies for greeting you like this, but when I looked out and saw the traffic I didn't know when you'd be arriving—"

"I'm glad you could enjoy yourself while waiting," she said.

"Let me just walk through the shower," he said, heading for a door as Seana nodded. Chi bowed and exited.

"Would you like a drink, Miss?" the butler Cholmondeley, pronounced Chumley, asked.

"A glass of champagne, please." The butler bowed out. Seana straightened herself in mirrors to her right and left, and looked systematically at everything in the room.

The butler returned with a champagne flute on a silver tray and served it to her. She took it gratefully and sipped. The butler bowed out. Mann entered, naked and wet, drying himself with a towel. She turned away demurely, amused. She kept her eyes on the Nautilus equipment and couldn't see him in the mirrors until she saw his hand lifting her glass of champagne. She spun around and was amazed to see him in a tuxedo, with perfectly made bow tie, taking a sip of her drink.

"How—how did you get all those clothes on so quickly?"

"Oh, I have my little ways," Ari said, gloating.

He escorted her to the huge sunken living room overlooking Park Avenue, where traffic was still stalled. The butler reappeared with two fresh glasses of champagne, bowing out as they clinked.

"To us," Mann said.

"Us," Seana said.

They sipped.

He looked down at the traffic. Two gunshots rang out but since gunfire happened every day nowadays, no one made mention of it. "Still Friday rush hour... care to see the rest of the place?"

"Sure."

He escorted her into the next room, an electronic office with computer screens everywhere. On the largest screen, a muted business news channel displayed acronyms and prices scrolling across the bottom.

"This is where I continue to redouble my self-made fortune," he said with surprising ego, stating it as a fact with a wry smile at himself.

He led her to an adjacent room, which contained a large Jacuzzi, massage table, and sensory deprivation tank, with New Age music complementing the scene.

"I shouldn't say 'self-made'... this is the room where I go to receive the fabulous tips someone has been giving me all my life." Mann said, now seeming authentic. "I call it my Receiving Room.

"When I read the TIME article about you taking over Wall Street, a little voice in my head said you were a psychic," Seana said.

"You hear little voices too!" he exclaimed with pleasure, and she nodded.

He took her into the next room, a huge library, and the next one, containing dart board and arcade videogames including some with light guns.

"The fun room," he said. Putting down his glass, he switched on a nearby videogame. Enemy spacecraft appeared and began to attack the player's spacecraft. Mann dispatched them all in a flash and switched on the next game. He played both games at the same time brilliantly then turned to a third one. Playing three games at the same time, he won them all, and finished up by whirling and throwing a dart he palmed into the triples ring. The dart whizzed by not far in front of Seana's face and she hopped back, spilling a single drop of champagne of the carpet.

"Sorry—didn't mean to scare you," he said.

"You didn't," she said honestly, thinking him infantile but giving no hint.

The butler appeared with fresh glasses and as he made his exit, he sprayed spot remover on the one drop of champagne on the carpet.

Mann took her into the next room, a ballroom, in the corner of which was a bandstand set up with instruments. They saw the brilliant lights of New York through the dominant south-facing window as dusk approached. Ari sat down at the piano and she stood a few feet away. He began to play and sing. He was superb.

"You go to my head..." She smiled at him appreciatively. A moment later she saw a gauzy image he must have projected of the two of them in bed making love, her body undulating powerfully. Her eyes widened. *"...and you linger like a haunting refrain..."* Seana felt ghostly fingers moving up and down her body. She stepped back uncomfortably. *"...and I find you going round in my brain like the bubbles in a glass of champagne..."* He stood up and finished his glass in a single move, picked up and began playing the sax, moving over to her so that she could feel the sound vibrations hitting her body. He played a few bars then resumed singing.

"...You intoxicate my soul with your thighs..." inserting his hand, he touched both of her white thighs at once and she pulled away, half-smiling. Mann put down the sax and gestured toward the French doors. "Traffic still sucks. But *they've* just given me a great idea," he said, texting something.

He led her out the French doors onto the giant terrace—the entire roof of the building not taken up by his suite. A lighted mosaic-tiled pool dominated half the terrace, surrounded by several chaise lounges, deck chairs and umbrella-covered tables. The other half of the terrace featured a large tiled area inlaid with strange markings. As they emerged onto the terrace, they saw the helicopter already approaching then landing precisely onto the inlaid markings. Mann helped Seana aboard and the helicopter took off again.

Fascinated but unafraid as the helicopter edged off the building, Seana looked down at the deep crevices called streets.

It was a very short hop down Park Avenue to the Met Life building, which had recently reopened its famous Copter Club decades after an ill-fated accident had shut it down. Ari bribed the pilot to let him make the landing which he did as expertly as he seemingly did everything else.

They were ushered inside like royalty by a number of seeming lords-and-ladies-in-waiting—and given the best table in the house, on a small stage from which they could see both rivers. The champagne continued to flow and then came the many courses of exquisite cuisine.

"So—at the McKenzie party, I didn't learn much about you," Ari said, drinking in her beauty as if he owned it.

"Your date didn't like me much," Seana teased, her eyes playful.

"How come you were the only unattached female there?"

"No one I wanted to go with."

"You give tarot readings for lots of rich people—that must be how you know Mrs. McKenzie?"

"Nice woman," Seana said authentically.

He seemed to agree, though his body language suggested certain reservations. "Hmm..." starting out ambiguously and then finding something good to say. "I like her society *balls*."

They were enjoying a first course of lobster something, with a white wine pairing.

"I had a secretary check the original guest list for the McKenzie party... you weren't on it..." he disclosed between bites.

She stopped in mid-mouthful.

"Why were you checking me?" she asked with a calm smile.

"The only unattached woman... I've got to suspect the motives of a woman who tries to meet me. Sorry if that seems... cold. I can assure you my feelings toward you are anything but. Please don't be offended. I'm a straight-up person, I just say what I think."

"You *are* psychic... I asked to be put on that guest list... I *did* want to meet you," Seana revealed, also between bites.

"Why? All the usual reasons, like my money?"

"No," she improvised. "I'm attracted to geniuses, it's the pattern of all my relationships."

"You're a genius groupie," he said and smiled affectionately, his paranoia significantly abated for the moment.

"Actually, more psychics than geniuses," she reflected. "TIME says they call you 'Mr. Brain' on Wall Street... I'm looking for 'Mr. Superhuman'..."

"How do I stack up so far?"

"I'm very interested," she said and managed to seem to mean it, even to his discerning extra senses.

"Good. I admire good taste," he said.

Accumulations of alcohol and perhaps whatever he might have slipped her caused great gaps in her memory of the rest of that night. She retained awareness of dancing at El Morocco, where a Latin band played and they danced the guajira. He was a professional level ballroom dancer of course. She appeared to be one too, so well did she follow his strong lead. He shamelessly sported an erection in his pants, grinding it against her as he held her tightly to his body. She was only slightly aroused but pretended more.

"You dance beautifully—just like you do everything else," she said.

"You haven't experienced how I do everything else... yet."

She sensed them in bed together for a fleeting instant. *Did he plant that image?* She made sure not to think in words because that was the easiest way to get read.

"No one's ever followed my lead so well," he said truthfully.

The next morning, she also remembered the two of them had somehow landed in the Jacuzzi, both wearing their respective form of panties. She had been wearing one of his shirts. She remembered lazily sticking her toes out of the bubbling water and looking at them, at which point she remembered herself saying, "It's getting late. I've had a wonderful time... I don't want the night to end, but I've got to give a reading in the morning..."

Then she remembered him helping her out of the Jacuzzi, taking her in his arms and kissing her passionately. She had responded in kind. As their lips parted, she had stepped back and he had grabbed her hand.

She remembered smiling softly and heard herself saying, "Not all at once." This recollection came with a sigh of relief.

He had smiled softly too, softening the grip on her hand. "I like it that way too."

The next morning in Shannon's office, Seana reported to Shannon and Williams.

"*The* most arrogant bastard—and I thought Jason Page was arrogant—" Seana began but Shannon, looking pained, waved for her to keep her voice down. She went on in a very low but audible voice, "No matter what you guys tell me I have to do with him, I hate his guts—"

Ω

Templegard was on a hospital ship under sedation, having been treated for extensive wounds. His dreaming consciousness was aboard the spaceship with his friends and comrades in this mission, whatever it was. He felt happy. The spaceship seemed to be heaving like a ship on the waters but he liked that too. Through the big transparent dome, he and all his friends now marveled at seeing *six* planets roughly lined up from Saturn to Mercury, including Earth, pointing at the center of the Milky Way. This was it. He didn't know what "it" was but he knew it would be big and it would be good. It was something they had all longed for—for a very long time.

Ω

Deep beneath the Ural Mountains, Nastassia wakened and sat up in bed with a curious expression. She got out of bed quietly and dressed rapidly. Minutes later she moved down a tunnel to an elevator and pressed the call button; moments later the door opened. An armed guard stood in the elevator, with his gun aimed at her.

"Not allowed," he stated.

"You're going up there anyway," she said, "couldn't I just ride with you—I need to see the sky—the guards let me." She made herself seem like a little girl far from home and afraid to never see the sky again. The guard could not picture her as a vulnerable little girl, especially since he had a crush on her, but he acquiesced and let her ride with him.

Shortly they were above ground and outside, the guard checking the perimeter, and she standing and hugging herself against the cold wind to look up at the sky. She at first saw nothing unusual. "Just a dream," she said to herself.

Then as her eyes panned around toward the center of the Milky Way, the curvy planetary lineup came into her view. "No... it wasn't..." she almost gasped in wonder.

Ω

At the same moment in New York, in the field headquarters of Theta Force, Shannon sat on the observer side of the one-way mirror looking out at the exercise room, where Williams, Seana, Khan and Page sat in lotus position, wearing headsets, their eyes seemingly looking inward, with Khan spinning a Tibetan Prayer Wheel, and hypnotic Northern Indian chants droning from the speakers.

Williams could see the four of them reflected in the mirror he faced. Then he heard an androgynous voice in his mind say, "The self sees itself as dwelling inside." He contemplated that for a moment. *Yes, my self seems to me to be behind my eyes,* he thought, although not in words.

His perspective then changed in an unusual way. He seemed to pull back and up from out of himself, and found himself looking down at the backs of the four of them, including himself. The voice then said, "Or the self sees itself as dwelling everywhere." Williams pondered that for a moment.

No, he couldn't remember ever picturing himself dwelling everywhere, but now he could, now that his awareness hovered outside of himself.

Shannon's voice came softly in his ear through the headset. "Marty, please report."

Shannon observed Williams stand and leave the exercise room while the others continued to concentrate. The door opened and Williams came in. He gave off a strong energy that put Shannon on alert. Williams sat down and said, forming each word with difficulty, "High... hard to talk."

"You take anything?" Shannon asked. Williams shook his head.

"Beyond words... don't lose by wording... *different*," Williams said.

Shannon stared at him. "Forget the training schedule," he said.

Williams returned to the exercise room and took his seat. Again, he saw the reflection in the mirror of the four of them concentrating. He suddenly heard himself think the words, *We had to give up psychic powers to use words.*

Only at first, said the androgynous voice.

Williams suddenly saw a vision of an undersea plant, each spiky branch having a shrewd-looking human face at the tip of it. A hundred cunning faces filled the screen of his mind.

You wonder who I am, the androgynous voice said. *Think about this: how can intelligence emerge at the part...*

Williams now saw his undersea plant as if he were trucking back from it. Looked at from further away, it formed a stupid-looking face.

And not at the whole?

Whoever was taking Williams on this journey now showed him empty space. The exercise room was gone. There were no stars. As he looked around, Williams' eyes fell on his image of God: light shining from Him, long-flowing beard, Grecian robe and sandals.

Life, a drug, you, as God, take...

God pops a pill and winks at Williams.

To forget you're alone... a trip away from Oneness.

God swoons.

Looking where he just saw God swoon, Williams now sees a male figure in bed, turning over, waking up, sitting up. He recognizes the figure as himself.

In the observer room, Shannon sees all four of the sitters looking stunned. The Prayer Wheel is still spinning and the deep voices are still chanting. He sees Williams look at the others questioningly and they all nod. Shannon touches his Bluetooth. "Marty, please report."

Moments later, Williams joins Shannon in the observer room.

"We're receiving," Williams said, "some sort of transmission... I think we're all getting it."

"How do you know?"

"The four of us... feel like one."

"Why today more so than any other day?"

"Seems we've turned some corner."

Ω

Half a planet away Nastassia lay wired up, alone in the nearly-featureless testing room.

"Same assignment," her boss Karesky said gruffly through the speakers.

"Locate the top brass of the American psychic force," Nastassia confirmed.

"Right. Theta Force."

Nastassia closed her eyes, going directly into a trance-like state.

"Stronger today..." she noted. "I've been feeling this... they are in two places..."

"Where is the leader?"

"Body of water..." Nastassia began.

"Which one?"

"Ocean... harbor..."

In the adjacent observer room, General Nikolai Karesky, head of Psychotronic Division One, watched her on a video monitor, along with an aide. Karesky flicked off the mic.

"We've waited so long... could this really be happening now?" the General mused aloud.

"Northern port..." Nastassia's voice came over the speakers.

The aide watched an EEG PET fMRI screen. "Brainwaves consistent with psychic performance," the aide reported. "Highest in the theta band. Left-right symmetry. Serotonin and oxytocin."

"Why today?" Karesky asked himself. "Like flicking a switch."

4

Back at Theta's field base in New York, the observer room was dark and empty. Shannon had joined the other four in the exercise room. All eyes were closed. The loud deep-throated chanting came through the speakers. Khan's Prayer Wheel continued to spin. Overwhelmed by the tidal wave of psychic energy from somewhere, all of them now watched and listened to a message from someone that each of them saw and heard somewhat differently.

Seana saw an Escher-like grid of bubbles going off in all directions, with a different dreamer in each bubble, wired to a dream machine. As she watched, she seemed to be zooming back and the bubbles all became cells in the body of a giant dreamer.

Williams broke out of his meditation to turn to Seana, just as she turned to him. "Unity," he said to her. She smiled and signaled assent with a single nod.

Shannon broke meditation to watch them. From his perspective, everything in the room appeared cellularized, breathing, but of one piece.

Williams turned to look at Shannon. From his point of view, he saw what Shannon saw: all of them as one connected thing, stitched into the spacetime from which they had sprung.

Shannon, still out of meditation, turned to Williams and Seana, and managed to form words. "Where... coming from," he asked with effort.

Seana pointed upward. "UFO?" she asked.

Williams barely shrugged and the three returned to meditation.

With his eyes open though attention turned inward, Williams saw the lights in the room seem to dim. In front of him, in the mirror, he could see the five of them meditating, Khan still spinning the Prayer Wheel. The other figures in the mirror seemed to dim but his own image alone still seemed to be brightly lit. Suddenly his image began to morph and although his features and body seemed to stay about the same, his clothing and appearance were morphing. He now presented as an African shaman in the era of cavemen. A second later, he appeared to be the high priest of Atlantis dressed in colorful feathers. He became many things very quickly and could only catch a few of them: Persian king, Pope, Druid, Minuteman of the American Revolution, robber baron, World War One Doughboy. Then he appeared as himself again.

The androgynous voice said to him, *In all of those lives you have been working toward the same purpose.*

Awestruck in sudden existential confusion, Williams realized someone was trying to remind him of some hidden truth. He vaguely remembered *something* but it was fleeting. Something was there but he couldn't see it, he could only sense it.

Khan was in a state of deep trance in which time seemed to stand still. The Prayer Wheel seemed to be going around and around by itself. He no longer heard the chanting. Though unfocused, his eyes could see the reflections of himself and his colleagues in the mirror. The room and everything in it appeared to be a single thing, made out of something gelatinous, with an underwater look. He could see bright subatomic particles of all colors showering down from above like meteorites of light, making electrical beeping sounds as they passed through and around him.

Jason Page, in deep space, watched God presenting as a Black woman. She began a medicine dance, and a pentagram-inlaid planet-like sphere appeared beneath her feet, absorbing the beating footfalls of her dance. Spinning like a dervish, She cast a spell on Herself, fell down, and got up as Jason Page.

An androgynous voice spoke in Jason's mind. *Each of us is God.*

Strange television sets appeared in space and showed him rapid-fire scenes of human disasters around the world being reported on a variety of news programs. *And yet we suffer,* the voice went on.

He heard an old reggae song, "Wild Goose Chase", and remembered his grandparents playing it when he visited them as a child in Harlem. Then he saw two lines of Black women dressed as Carmen Miranda dance past him on either side, singing one line of that song over and over again, "Who will save the human race?" Then all images and sound faded and he was alone in space again.

"I don't have the power!" Jason heard himself say, although no one else in the room heard him speak at all.

Yes, you do, the androgynous voice said.

Space all around him became a sphere of mirrors where he saw himself reflected no matter where he looked. Always Black, he watched himself change into a graceful apelike creature with a high forehead, an Egyptian priest, Ham the son of Noah, Amenhotep III, Ramses II, Zarathustra, Buddha, Plato, and Jesus, suffering on the cross. In shock he suddenly heard the horrible raucous cries of the crowd at Golgotha. He looked down and locked eyes with a woman he vaguely remembered but didn't know from where or when. It was Nastassia. He saw her as his wife, Mary Magdalene.

"Oh my God, I was Jesus!" he screamed, bursting into tears, but no one heard him. For the others, he was in meditation with his eyes closed and a strange expression on his face, looking therefore just like them.

Ω

On the other side of the world, a frozen tableau of stopped time existed for Nastassia. She had her lips pursed as if to speak but had stopped in mid-breath. She couldn't see but sensed that those in the next room observing her had also frozen in time, that the whole universe stood still, outside of time. She had stopped breathing but that didn't bother her.

Transported into space, she found herself in a room with transparent walls. Outside her room, other rooms—all with transparent walls—went off in all directions forever. She could see the immobile Karesky and his aide in the observation room next door. Beyond that room she saw the Theta operatives frozen in meditation in their exercise room. In another direction she saw Ari Mann's Jacuzzi room, with Ari in the Jacuzzi. Above her, a room in a Tibetan temple looked over a huge distant valley. There sat a young Lama she did not recognize, although most people in the world knew the boy from his many television appearances as the Danang Lama, a gifted Vietnamese psychic identified in Tibet as a Lama. Since there was no access to outside television in the Psycho base except as assigned for a mission purpose, Nastassia couldn't have known the Danang Lama.

Now transported into a French castle, she looked down at her colorful Renaissance garb. In front of her a portico with an arched top looked out on a beautiful countryside. I *remember this life now,* she heard herself think in words. *My name was Nicole then but everyone called me Nikki.* But as memories of that life trickled into her mind, she realized that she had not been with the man from her dreams in this life. She wondered, then, why she was being shown this life in particular.

Ω

Alone in his Jacuzzi listening for "hot tips", Ari Mann suddenly laughed wildly. "They've stepped up the power on us!"

Ari suddenly saw appear before him a window, arched on top, square on bottom, through which he was staring at Nastassia, who was staring back at him. *This was a lover of mine in another life long ago,* he guessed uncertainly.

Ari disappeared to Nastassia, and now through the same window she saw Jason. His eyes and hers became tender as they recognized each other as the lovers they had once been.

"You... I... how forgotten..." Page said to her, barely able to form his words.

"Our paths... diverged," she managed to respond. She wanted to let him down gently. He was not her destined mate. The man from her dreams was her destiny.

He reached out to touch her face. There was an electrical sparking sound as she and the window disappeared.

Ω

Karesky and his aide, unaware that time had stopped, were concerned when Nastassia did not reply to them and so rushed into the room where she lay wired up. They found her seemingly not breathing and called for a doctor, who soon arrived and took some instrument readings. They all jumped as she began to speak from her trance state.

"This is the time of alignment... we have returned... to help the butterfly emerge," she said slowly. Then she went silent again. The men shot glances at each other. The aide and the doctor sensed an explosion building up in Karesky.

Nastassia's eyes fluttered open and she took in the others with surprise. "Did I fall asleep again? I had visions—" she began.

"You were talking in your sleep," Karesky said, and she detected some warning in the way he spoke.

"What did I say?" she asked cautiously. She hoped she had not said anything that sounded religious to Karesky. She imagined him capable of delivering great punishments and feared for her parents, given his past admonishments.

"We'll get it transcribed," he said evasively, locking eyes momentarily with the aide who then nodded. "Seems to be a message... from somebody to somebody," he went on, taking to a chair. He then signaled to the doctor, who reflexively began taking her pulse. The aide also sat down and took out his tablet to take readings from Nastassia's brain. The screen still showed the configuration for high psychic performance. She seemed normal now yet was still in her psychic space. The aide showed the screen to Karesky who quickly got it and turned back to question Nastassia.

"Yes... it is a message," Nastassia said. "Not just for us... heard by all psychics everywhere on Earth I think."

Karesky's face darkened. "Heard by Theta Force?" he asked urgently.

"I'm sure they would have gotten it... our psychic troops too," she said.

"Check it out," he snapped to his aide, who then started to stand. "No, after this," Karesky clarified and the aide sat back down. "Why do you think someone else beside you got this message?" he asked Nastassia.

"Very powerful... the most powerful experience I've ever had," she divulged.

"Why today, do you suppose?" Karesky asked nervously, scratching his ear.

"I think..." Nastassia started and chose her words cautiously to avoid a Karesky blowup, "we've entered a special time."

He pounced. "The 'Time of Alignment'?" Karesky asked, and she gave him a shocked look. "You said something like that in trance. Mean anything to you?" he prompted.

"Last night I dreamed there was a lineup of stars—" she began to confess her ride to the surface.

"Is that why you went up to the surface, to see if the lineup was really there?" Karesky asked malevolently.

"You found out—" Nastassia blurted.

"The guard has already been disciplined," Karesky said with a vicious smile, and she looked and felt guilty for whatever punishment befell the guard. "You have cut a wide swath through my troops with your antics, Lieutenant. So did you see your lineup?"

"I saw it."

The doctor stopped taking her pulse, tapped a note into his tablet, and began to listen to her body through his stethoscope.

The aide was watching his screen for signs of lying in the brain patterns.

"So many stars up there, it's easy to imagine them forming lines and patterns. Now I think our comrades in Moscow listening to this audio file will appreciate not having to listen to any more astrological horseshit, don't you?"

She nodded guardedly.

"We started this session with an assignment," he went on. "What can you tell me about the location of the Theta Force commander?"

"Northern port... is New York," she said.

The aide, reading from his display, said, "Could be a lie."

Briefly furious, Nastassia instantly brought herself out of her trance. "Why would I lie?!" She had never lied. However, she could mislead people quite well when she needed to, without lying. She felt she would never let herself actually lie.

The doctor ripped the stethoscope from his ears as he jumped back.

"Sorry for raising my voice, doctor," she mumbled.

"I didn't say it was a lie, I'm just doing—" the aide objected, wanting her to like him.

"Shut up," Karesky ordered, and then to Nastassia he said, "He's just doing his job. Are you sure it's New York?"

"Yes," she said with certainty. She started to explain why she was so certain but something deep inside stopped her. Still high from *The Message*, she had heard a male voice say "New York" right after she had seen two of her past life lovers, though neither was her dream man. She didn't know which one had said it to her, but it felt like someone had put a scrap of paper with a telephone number on it into her hand.

"Mission accomplished, then," Karesky said suddenly in a much better mood, and nodding with his compatriots. "Feels nice to say *that* for a change," he added authentically and then regretted having said something defeatist before witnesses.

"This is Berla..." boomed the voice of Field Marshall Berla over the speaker.

Karesky, who reported to Berla, became instantly silent.

"I have been taking a keen interest in these proceedings since your officer of the watch called to ask me if you should be interrupted. I told him no," Berla said.

"Why did he call you, sir?" Karesky asked meekly.

"A number of your troops reported receiving some sort of transmission. General, please clear the room except for the Lieutenant and yourself," Berla commanded.

Karesky gestured with his eyes and the doctor and aide swiftly left.

"We're alone, sir," Karesky reported.

"Comrades, I've already reported to the top," Berla confided. "The word is that, whoever just sent that transmission, and whatever they are trying to tell us—they've just demonstrated a new level of psychic power—a broadcast we don't know how many people heard. Our people must connect to that source before the Americans do."

5

Dripping wet, Ari wrapped himself in a large towel and went to his tablet to make a call. He heard rings and then the pickup of an automated messaging system without a welcoming message. He spoke after the beep. "This is Mann. I need to see you. Anyplace but here—"

He noticed there had been a second beep right before his last two words. He wondered if Otto had a way of cutting off messages at exactly the right point to give him free reign to do as he pleased. *That would be a useful device, perhaps I should invent it,* Ari thought.

At the home of Otto Wagner, an exceptionally tall visitor observed with amusement Otto's prank with the programmable answering system. Otto, a bald, bullet-headed though not unattractive middle-aged man in a double-breasted suit, looked up at the man adoringly, pleased with the implied praise. Otto knew his visitor was not actually a man, or even human, despite looking exactly like a certain historical figure.

Ω

The droning chanting had been turned off. The Prayer Wheel lay on its side on the padded floor. Most of the participants also laid on their sides or sat cross-legged, all looking stunned. Khan spoke first.

"Did... you all hear it too?" he asked. After an instant's pause, the others broke out in laughter, and a moment later Khan too laughed at his own innocence. They wiped away tears.

"Somebody is trying to tell us something," Shannon stated the least ambiguous thing he could think of, reaching for a mooring.

"That somebody... is almost certainly not an Earth human," Seana offered.

Shannon laughed unsurely. "What makes you say that?"

"None of us has that kind of power," Seana replied matter-of-factly.

Shannon shook his head as if to clear away a cobweb. "Let's try to deal with this without getting farfetched—" he began.

"I'd call what just happened pretty farfetched," Khan commented drily.

Shannon looked at Seana, trying to open his mind. "What do you mean, not an Earth human?" he asked her.

She shook her head and shrugged, her eyebrows raised. "I don't know, a UFO? Ascended Masters? Jesus coming back?"

Jason took a sharp audible in-breath and the others looked at him. He looked somewhat odd. In not quite his usual voice, he then said, "I didn't know... who I *was.*"

They stared at him, waiting for him to go on, but he didn't.

"What do you mean?" Shannon pressed him for more.

"I still have a mission here," Jason said.

Shannon seemed to be getting impatient. "Yes, you do, of course," he said, looking at all of them. "But what was the point of *The Message*?"

Williams seemed to still be on some kind of a high. "We're not really separate... we're all one thing together... all that exists is a single consciousness," he said.

The others noticed that Williams had completely changed. A radiant beatified expression had come over his face. They stared at him in shocked concern.

"Marty, are you okay?" Shannon asked.

"In the beginning there was God—a single Consciousness," Williams went on, as if he were channeling. "It created us and

It lives through each of us—each of us cells lives many lives, evolving from subatomic particles up through plant, animal and human levels to even higher levels—until we remember ourselves as God again—"

Seana did not recognize this Williams and tried to reassure herself by making light of his words. "Who is in there?" she asked playfully, looking into his eyes.

Jason answered her question strangely, saying, "He's a psychic vampire! The Logos is supposed to be coming through me—he's stealing my role—"

Shannon saw them all falling apart and took over. "At ease! We're all shaken up by what just happened—I suggest we chill out for a while. Written reports then—bring them here at five o'clock."

$$\Omega$$

The butler greeted Ari Mann as he entered his apartment. "Good evening, sir—Mr. Wagner is waiting for you in your office. With a gift, sir," he announced.

"Really," Ari said, clearly irritated.

Proceeding into his office, he saw Otto drinking a high-ball, sitting in a Gothic-looking ornately-carved chair that had never been there before.

"Otto," Ari said levelly.

Otto got up and they embraced coldly. "Ari," Otto said.

"I thought my message made it clear to meet anywhere but here," Ari said.

"My answering system must have cut that part off," Otto lied.

"Sure," Ari feigned agreement. He indicated the chair. "A gift?" he asked.

"Something you will be needing," Otto advised him.

"Needing," Ari said sarcastically.

Otto sat back in the chair with a smile. "Ah, Mr. Brain, do I detect more than your usual trace of arrogant disbelief in my powers? When I found you, you didn't even know you had them too," he advised Ari.

Ari sat behind his desk. "Yes. I'll bet you even picked up why I wanted to see you."

"I received the same boosted-power transmission," Otto said flatly.

"Of course you did," Ari replied unsurprised. "Where was it from?"

Otto became angry. "Where do you think it was from? It was from The Leaders."

Ari appeared unconvinced but quickly hid his doubts. "Just checking. You hadn't told me it was coming. Its purpose?"

"As with any action, our purpose is to hasten evolution. As I've hastened yours, and continue to," Otto proclaimed.

"Hmm. What about the chair, then—Its purpose?" Ari inquired.

"Ah," Otto said and stood. "Press the button."

Still feeling irritable, Ari started, "What b—" then stopped to feel under his desk and sure enough there was a matchbook-sized object that had been affixed there, from which a button protruded. "No wires... radio frequency," Ari concluded and Otto nodded, pleased. "Triggers some sort of restraint system in the chair..." Ari guessed and pressed the button. A needle popped up through the seat where it would puncture the occupant's right buttock. Ari was aghast. "Barbarous... what's in the needle?" he demanded.

"Just a restraint system, as you said," Otto responded coolly.

"I don't want this sick thing in my home," Ari stated point-blank.

"I think you'll find this is covered in our contract," Otto said, confident of his upper hand.

Ari was quiet a moment. "All right," he gave in. "But I don't see why."

Otto spoke lovingly to the chair as he reached under the seat and re-cocked the mechanism, taking the needle out of sight once again. "So ungrateful, isn't he, my lovely? You'll be needing this needle," he said to Ari, his disproportionate laugh echoing strangely in Ari's ears.

Ω

In his room Jason sat writing on his tablet. *If—no "if"—I was Jesus Christ. That means my life... now... must be The Second Coming.* He stopped writing. *But how can I tell you people that? You'll think I've snapped.* Looking at his watch, he saw that his written report was due in ten minutes. He got up and began to pace the room.

Jason's father was a famous basketball star, now retired to doing TV commercials and looking for movie roles. A middle child in a large family, Jason lived large as kin to a world class celebrity. Despite being spoiled, he always felt that he never got to be the star of anything. Never got the recognition that he deserved. Although other people seemed to never see it, Jason could tell that he was better than other people, morally and intellectually. Somehow his good grades and good looks, which should have won public adulation, were not paying off for him as he thought they should—as if he was cursed by some unnatural force. A murderous rage burned inside him against this suspected outside agent that blinded people to his exceptional qualities.

When he learned martial arts, he found at least there he could earn higher level belts, which he did and wore as badges of his distinction. When he found that he could fight blindfolded and was extremely good at it, he began to feel that his life was finally turning out all right. But that skill led to his being recruited into Theta Force by Khan, who had taught him blindfold fighting in the first place. So even in that special skill he was still not number one in anything.

The Message came to Jason at a time in his life when he had actually considered killing himself. Now, in place of suicidal thinking, he had the ultimate coming true of his deepest wish to be applauded for his unequalled specialness. And seeing an extravagantly beautiful lover of his from another lifetime come back into his life, surely this must be a sign that this was indeed his special time.

That would have been ecstasy.

The agony came in not knowing how to tell anyone without having to suffer even greater ridicule.

Ω

In the conference room, Shannon, Williams, Seana, Jason and Khan had been reading each other's reports on their respective devices. One by one they finished reading and looked up. Shannon waited until everyone was ready.

"So many visions," he began. "Where's the common thread?" He looked around and for a moment it seemed no one was going to answer.

"Although we think of ourselves as separate beings," Williams, with a steady smile, responded calmly, "that is actually an illusion. All there is here is One Being masquerading as many."

They stared at him.

"One incorporeal psychic Being—why not just call him/her by some name—how about 'God'? God sends a piece of His/Her mind off on a trip, cut off from memory of being God, to live many lives and through these evolve up to re-merge with the Original Identity, bringing many photo albums of experience to enhance and/or entertain the Original Identity."

"That may have been it," Seana acknowledged, "most of it..."

Khan tentatively nodded.

"But we obviously all *are* separate—" Shannon started to say.

"You saw the visions, too." Williams pointed out. "Obviously anything can be presented to us so we see it in full clarity, as if it were reality. So this reality we see now is just itself one long vision..."

"Marty," Shannon said sympathetically, "you sound like you're still a little weird in the head... still tripped out from your trance-meditation."

Williams looked at Seana as if expecting to see support in her eyes but didn't. He went on confidently, "I have the feeling that I knew this *Message* before but somehow forgot it—it feels as if a part of myself that has been suppressed for a very long time is now remembering..."

"This is getting freaky," Shannon said, and everyone nodded, including Seana. "Can we stick to the possible military significance? I've reported this to the top and all they can think is that this has got to be the Russians monkeying around... with some device that can magnify thoughts... DARPA thinks maybe something derived from the Tesla technology..."

Williams laughed.

"If the Russians can do anything like this, we might as well give up now," Khan said, mostly in disbelief and thus in jest.

"The military significance," Williams said, "is that some of the escalating wars now being fought are between Muslims and Jews and Christians, or between Muslims and Hindus. If the human race really got this *Message*, it would wind down those wars, maybe *all* wars."

"I don't see it," Shannon said.

"Don't you?" Williams persisted. "*The Message* has come through before. The Invisible Being spoke to Abraham and Moses and Isaiah, and to Buddha and Jesus and Mohammed and countless others just as it spoke to us today. They must have found it just as hard to put into words as we do—even harder because they were less sophisticated in the use of language. The message of Oneness got garbled into so many different forms that it started different religions, which are now competing with each other."

"That's pretty dismissive of Christianity," Jason said.

"Congratulations, Martin," Khan added, "you have just managed to insult all of the religions at once." He was kidding but it seemed otherwise.

"Marty," Seana said caringly, "I think that kind of talk is more likely to start another religious war than to end one."

"*The Message* doesn't obsolete all the religions," Williams pointed out, "it explains their underlying unity. And for those without religion it offers a scientific explanation for why fighting with each other—or fighting others—is like fighting with yourself."

Could this be my mission? Williams mused. *To describe my experience of The Message so well that it changes every-one the way it has changed me?* That seemed ridiculously unlikely. Maybe he would have to keep his revelation to him-self. But no, he had to at least share it with Theta, he could not hold back anything from them that might make their psychic powers increase—that was his job.

6

Karesky and Nastassia sat across from one another at Karesky's desk, on which lay the printed transcript of her official report. Karesky pointed at a passage.

"And this is the point at which the lie detector acted up," Karesky said. Their eyes met, she said nothing. He went on. "Tell me how it is that you knew the location was New York."

"I just knew, that's all," Nastassia said.

"Did you see the famous skyline? Was that it?" he pressed her.

"No, it was nothing I saw," she said.

"Then how did you know?"

She closed her eyes and paused. "The words 'New York' just seemed to come into my mind."

Karesky was suddenly more attentive. "What else did you experience at that point?"

"I saw a man... a Black man... who seemed familiar... and another man—"

Karesky flipped pages. "Yes... seeing each man through an archway, right?"

She nodded and opened her eyes.

"Who was this Black man?" Karesky pressed further.

"I don't know... I just know that we had been lovers—"

"You mean in a past life?" Karesky snorted.

She nodded tiredly.

49

"You know what I think of that stuff. You know what I think?" Showing his agitation, Karesky continued, "I think our Theta friends caused this whole incident."

Her eyes widened.

"Yes, I think they may have done all this to get you to go to New York—"

"General, with all due respect, the Americans could not have gone this far past us—"

"And the other man..." Karesky probed, ignoring her objection.

"I saw him relaxing in a big hot tub, in an expensive room full of expensive things. He must be a rich man. I never saw him before. I presume I saw him because he was also a previous lover... as it says in my report, General, sir."

"I want you to draw from memory what each man looked like," he commanded.

"Now?"

"Yes." He pressed a button. "Send in a large sketch pad and pencils right away."

He used the time waiting to stare at her loveliness while she stared at whorls in the pine desktop. His presence itself felt like browbeating to her. Deep inside she was unfazed but pretended to be frightened of him because he liked it.

Karesky's secretary, Tassie, brought in the art supplies. Nastassia would have liked to befriend Tassie, but the woman had been ordered not to fraternize with the Psycho troops. In fact, no one outside Psycho was allowed to talk to Psycho personnel beyond the basic necessities of daily life. To focus Psycho and keep it secret, they thought the best thing to do was to cut it off from outside contact except as necessary for external field missions.

Nastassia drew the faces of Jason and Ari side by side, going back and forth to add more strokes of her pencil on each picture. Karesky watched, flabbergasted at the sureness and speed with which she created two drawings that looked almost photographically real.

"What—are you a professional artist too?!" he managed to ask.

"No, sir," she replied, as surprised as he was. "This must be the result of the transmission, I'm changed in many ways. I could not draw like this before—I am not doing this drawing, it's doing itself..."

Ω

Jason was not listening to the discussion going on around him in the conference room. He was thinking about his psychic powers. Would they be as strong as when he was Jesus, so that he *would* be recognized? Was the childhood environment that never gave him his due capable of stifling his psychic powers to the degree that he would *not* be recognized? But if they had crushed his self-belief, knowing that now, why couldn't he snap his fingers and dispel those effects?

Something in the room caught his attention and he looked up. The others were all staring at him.

"What?" Page asked, somewhat defensively.

"I said," Shannon repeated, "the only one who saw someone they knew was Jason."

"That's true," Jason admitted, wondering where this was going to lead.

"Tim was just saying," Williams explained, "that if what we all heard was some sort of Russian transmission, maybe the woman who appeared to be a past lover was a ruse to get information out of you."

"Like maybe they hypnotized you with the suggestion that she was a past lover," Shannon elucidated further.

Williams, looking down on his tablet at Jason's report, added, "It says here that as the connection broke, you sent her 'New York' so she could find you."

Shannon locked eyes with Jason. "You could have just given away our position to an enemy agent. I thought you had been trained not to give information to someone you meet in your dreams."

Feeling flustered, Jason responded, "I'm sure she is a past lover... I had completely forgotten... when I saw her, all the memories came back in a rush. I sensed the connection would last only an instant—I had to do something—"

"Let's say she was a Russian," Shannon postulated. "The other agencies and the military personnel attached to our Moscow embassy have this trouble all the time with seductive Russian women. We haven't got the luxury of giving away our position just to keep someone's phone number—"

"That's not fair!" Jason retorted.

Ω

Ari had retired to his Jacuzzi after Otto left. *I'm not doubting you are The Leaders* he said in his mind, attempting direct communication in an end-around play, *I'm just questioning whether Otto really represents you... Why would you use needles rather than something psychic or at least electronic? He says it's just to knock someone out but he's crazy, this guy Otto, maybe this would kill somebody... an untraceable poison, just a little sting mark on the ass... am I going to have to get rid of a body so that it can't be traced to me and that chair? What am I being set up for? What kind of a test is this and how do I win it?*

Ω

Everyone in the conference room was talking at once when the phone rang. They fell silent as Shannon picked it up.

"Shannon here." Tim listened for a moment. "Okay, send it up." He clicked off. He got up and stepped over to the wall, where he slid open a panel exposing a giant screen, which came on and adjusted itself. "Headquarters is sending us a video," he explained, "out of the evening network news," he looked at his watch, "about a half hour ago."

The smirking newsman appeared at his desk. "And here's today's wildest story: psychics all over the world have reported receiving a transmission today, all at exactly the same time, which was 11:11 AM here on the East Coast when it started and exactly noon when it ended."

"Wow!" Seana exclaimed.

"There's a lot of disagreement," the newscaster went on, "about exactly what *The Message* said, but most psychics are in agreement that it seemed to be a spiritual message, something about each of us being part of God."

"Kind of rules out the Russians, *n'est-ce pas*?" Williams asked.

"The National Enquirer and the National Star," the newsman continued, "have both announced that they have so many call-ins, they will be publishing special editions covering the incident. NBS's Donald Samuelson was at the White House when we received the news, and he got this statement from the President."

The picture switched to the White House lawn, where earlier that day Samuelson held a mic near the President's face, with Secret Service agents crowded close by.

"Well, I've actually known about this for a couple of hours," President Gomez, who looked like a friendly schoolteacher, said. "We've had our own level-headed people taking a hard-nosed look at these phenomena for some time."

"That must be us. Yay team!" Seana expostulated.

"I got their report during lunch today that something unusual had transpired," the president said and nodded sagely. "We'll be checking it out to see if there's anything to it."

The monitor cut back to the newsman at his desk and went black. The monitor then turned itself off and Shannon slid the panel closed. "That's it," he said.

"Would be nice if he'd kind of come out of the closet about us a bit more," Seana dreamed aloud.

"Guess we need a few more square people to die before he can do that," Jason said cynically.

"That's a very Christian thing to say," Seana replied sarcastically.

"Even Jesus said that not everyone can get into heaven," Jason countered.

"Not right away, maybe," Williams said, "but eventually we all get there—because we're all from there."

"I guess you're putting yourself above Jesus," Jason said.

"No, never," Williams said. "But his followers let him down by making everyone think that only *he* was God Incarnate— *The Message* says that *everybody* is. If Jesus had lived longer, he might have given us the message we heard today—if and when he thought we were ready for it."

"At ease!" Shannon said sharply. "Okay, maybe it wasn't the Russians—but they know about it. We've got to be first to find the source."

Ω

Shannon was alone in his office studying Internet news reports of *The Message* and hoping for a flash of insight when his young assistant Donna knocked. "Come!" he said and she stuck her head in.

Donna had just graduated from the Point with top honors in physics. Since the formation of Theta Force the Army had begun routinely testing its personnel for psychic powers, without revealing the purpose of the testing. She had been discovered to be an adept. Her psychic powers had clearly given her the ability to grasp the complexities of quantum physics and relativity. She had not been informed of how psychically powerful her test results showed her to be, and was assigned a relatively low position in Theta to prevent feeding her ego. Williams had been the first to realize, by introspection, that ego dissolved psychic powers. This discovery had been added to the Theta Force training manual, which was "eyes only" for a select few.

"Congressman Baynes on line one," Donna announced. Shannon picked up the phone and she closed his door and returned to the receptionist's desk guarding the entrance.

"Yes, sir," Shannon said into the phone.

Baynes was in his own office in DC, all oak and leather looking slightly dusty and worn like the Congressman himself. "Must say, son, the timing of this *Message* couldn't have worked out better for you. You got an interim appropriation."

Shannon went from depression to euphoria in nothing flat. "Terrific! I know we owe you our thanks for that."

"It wasn't me this time, your *Message* was the magic," Baynes replied. "You know, I'm always suspicious when something *interesting* conveniently happens, right after someone's been threatened that they better show results soon—"

"Congressman, you can't be serious—"

"It just doesn't make a lot of sense to me," Baynes muttered. "Why would a more advanced civilization use such powerful technology to communicate with us, only to tell us such irrelevant nonsense?"

Shannon stifled a disbelieving laugh. "Well... it may not be of *military* significance..."

"How about Ari Mann," Baynes interrupted. "Is *he* of military significance?"

"I wouldn't know," Shannon said casually, deflecting Baynes' probe.

"Don't be coy, Colonel," Baynes retorted sharply. "I know he's the subject of your surveillance in New York. In fact I know a lot more about it now than you do."

"I wouldn't be surprised," Shannon said. "Some of the other agencies aren't all that cooperative with us..."

"They use the word 'voodoo' a lot when your name comes up," Baynes quipped.

Shannon didn't take the bait. "What do you know that I don't about Ari Mann?" he asked bluntly.

"A lot," Baynes bragged mysteriously, "but it all comes down to this: he's born a Russian, lives most of his young life an Israeli, and now he's an American. What does that say to you?"

"You're saying he's a spy," Shannon supplied.

"Patterns fit," Baynes agreed, "like this transmission of yours. Theta is at risk of being closed down, needs a field goal, the president has been using Theta for a personal vendetta against his harshest critic, gets caught—and bingo! *God talks to us,* Gomez' ass is saved, and your ass is saved."

Shannon was incredulous. "You think we just manipulated all the media stories?"

"That's a lot easier for me to swallow than your story that God or some Space Jesus spoke to us," Baynes laid out confidently.

"Congressman—this is crazy—" Shannon held up a news report on his tablet, although Baynes couldn't read it. "There are thousands of witnesses—"

Baynes made poo-pooing noises and Shannon began losing patience.

"Surely, you're aware, Mr. Baynes, that the Danang Lama also reported receiving the transmission, and is coming to the United Nations to explain its meaning?"

"How much did you have to pay him?" Baynes asked impertinently.

Shannon was speechless.

7

Karesky was uncomfortable sitting across the desk from Field Marshall Berla in the boss's office, where he usually got frying glances and worse. However, Berla today seemed merely impassive. Karesky did not let himself cheer up too much for fear of jinxing himself and copping a blast after all. He would be happy to get out of there hopefully soon and unscathed.

They had been talking about the recon to New York.

"You seem hesitant about sending Slayevsky," Berla challenged him.

"The lie detector indicated..." Karesky explained carefully, "that she might have her own reasons to want to go to New York."

"Like to defect?" Berla asked.

"She's never been much of a team player," Karesky said. He had been reporting this all along, since they brought her in two years ago at age thirteen but looking nineteen. She had not been promiscuous but was quite a flirt. Her big problem, reportedly, was her stubborn clinging to religious superstition, as her bosses thought of it. They didn't think they could beat it out of her so they hadn't tried that yet. They had only tenuous control over her even though she was terribly concerned about the safety and comfort of her parents, who were being held under guard in a safehouse.

"I want her under the tightest possible surveillance while she's over there, starting as soon as she leaves the base, and not lapsing until she returns," Berla ordered steely-eyed.

Karesky nodded, though he had his reservations. She was suspected to have more psychic power than any of the rest of the division. She had done a few things nobody else had ever done, such as the ability to make someone else have a momentary hallucination. And now this photographic-like drawing. What next? They needed to keep her on their side. At the same time, keeping her but not using her made no sense.

"Does it have to be her? She's too valuable to lose—" Karesky had the gumption to bring his concerns back up again. He saw her as his ticket to the top, which was transparent to Berla.

Berla didn't like giving Karesky more information than he felt necessary. He saw Karesky as the type who could subconsciously cause him some kind of embarrassment so that the man would get Berla's job in the end. But in this case the man had a need to know.

"No choice. We've got to send our best. Top is worried that this is for real... it fits the First Contact scenario. Almost all the psychics on our list are buying tickets to New York for a big meeting at the UN... now the Danang Lama..."

"Theta could be doing all this," Karesky blurted, immediately regretting it. But he didn't get snarled at this time, so counted his lucky stars.

"To get one of us, you mean," Berla interpreted.

"Right," Karesky said, feeling a rare sense of triumph: he actually gave the boss an idea.

"Before you let that happen," Berla said with bitter resignation, "better that she be dead."

Ω

Shannon sat alone in his office, still in disbelief of the degree to which a sane person could believe unbelievable scenarios. He also contemplated his next moves and Seana seemed to be the bishop he had to move next. He'd opened the door to let fresh air in and, moments later, Seana happened by and peeked in.

"How long you been thinking of me?" Seana asked cheerfully, somewhat pleased with herself.

Feeling pleased with her too, Shannon motioned her to come in and close the door. "Less than a minute," he replied.

She flashed a big smile at how quickly she had picked up on it and come by, presuming that he was summoning her, perhaps merely as a test.

"Hey I—" she began.

He put up his hand and she slapped it with a high five motion.

"I'm not going," she said and his face darkened. "Only kidding! You want me to go see Ari Mann again... something about the president..."

He nodded. He had continued to restrain himself, never letting it show how much he was attracted to her. He had fantasized marrying her—at least until she and Marty became an item. Part of him resisted sending her to see another man, knowing she might have to sleep with him. He'd also had visions of having worked with her in other lives, although he wasn't sure he believed in reincarnation.

Seana believed in reincarnation and felt quite sure she had worked with Shannon in prior lives. Sometimes she felt a certain attraction to him that was almost equal to what she felt for Marty. She had fantasized, *what if Shannon had made the first move rather than Marty?* But Shannon acted—well, not cold, but—very professional. He pretty much owned this Theta outfit and was responsible for it and for its protection of the free world, which didn't leave room for anything else, or at least that's the way it seemed to Seana. She also felt certain that she had worked with Marty in other lives, but something told her that maybe they hadn't been lovers until this time around.

Shannon and Seana looked at each other, sensing the other's reveries though careful not to cross the line into reading each other's minds. They each wondered how well they knew each other.

"Yes, but only if it comes up," Shannon said after what seemed like a long silence but was only seconds. "Find out why he hates the president."

"Otherwise?" Seana asked.

"Keep improving the relationship," he responded. "Say you just wanted to see him. Oh yeah—don't warn him you're coming—just walk in on him."

"*That* will improve the relationship," she said sarcastically.

"Everyone seems to know more than we do... we're going to have to start taking them off guard..." he said, repeating the president's words.

Ω

Ari reclined in his office chair, seemingly looking out the window at the late afternoon light, but actually looking inside at his latest idea about air conditioned clothing. He saw the flashing light on the intercom and tapped the key.

"Yes?" he said aloud.

"Mister Wagner and Ms. Moon have arrived, sir," Cholmondeley said through the speaker.

"What?! Arrived... together?" Ari's mind raced. *Was she an agent of Otto's all along?*

"They apparently met in the elevator, sir."

"Damn..."

Seana and Otto waited in the exercise room. Otto sat watching her work out on the butterfly machine, which she was doing to hide her nervousness. She could sense that Otto was telepathic—so now there were two of them, of unknown strength as psychics, she would be facing. She saw this as the first situation of what she considered to be danger that she had been put in since joining Theta. She felt on edge and called on her training to bolster her ability to act casually. The music suddenly came on and she recognized the old song, "She's an Airhead", and figured that was Ari's way of berating her for barging in on him.

Ari swept into the room in his usual style and saw her exercising. "Lift your mind and your tits will follow," he said, crassly referring to the bust exercise she was doing.

"So lift my mind already," she riposted. She offered her arms and he lifted her out of the seat with quick pecks on each cheek, then turned to coldly shake hands with Otto.

"The most amazing synchronicity, Ari," Otto said, "How often does someone drop in on you without calling first?"

"Never!" Ari exaggerated to make a point.

"Exactly!" Otto said. "And tonight, both Seana and I simultaneously got the impulse to just *come* see you. Incidentally, we made a very *deep* connection in the elevator." He turned to look at her admiringly and they all registered the intended double entendre.

After allowing an uncomfortable silence for a moment, Ari said hollowly, "Well, what a pleasure. Come, let's go out on the terrace."

Seana breathed deeply, controlling her fear, as they walked together down the long corridor lined with its fabulous statuary and paintings, this time with Ari telling her about certain pieces as they passed them. She was distracted by her thoughts, however. *He's furious that we dropped in but hiding it well. What power does Otto have over Ari?*

They emerged onto the terrace, at once feeling and smelling the warm flower-scented air and just barely hearing the crawling muted taxis honking far below. An umbrellaed table had been set for them by two waiters, who held their chairs out and seated them. As she came back to paying attention to the conversation, Seana heard Otto saying something seemingly about her.

"—the sensation of knowing somebody deeply although you've just met them."

She thought that he was thinking of sex when he used the word "deep" twice in such a short time, but then remonstrated herself that he could mean the practice of picking up quiet feelings deep inside, a phenomenon with which she was very familiar. The waiters brought them champagne and served Beluga caviar and pâté de foie gras.

Ari, trying to read their minds, not something he usually did, got a flash of the Hieronymus Bosch painting in his private elevator.

"It was the picture," Seana started to say.

"Yes," Otto said. "You know, Ari, your Bosch—we were both looking at it and then—"

"Each of us saw both of us in the painting," Seana concluded.

Ari had a brief picture in his mind of their faces on two of the bizarre characters in the painting.

"I felt her in my head—I knew she was psychic, too," Otto said.

"Well, why do you think I have that thing in my elevator?" Ari kidded. "I hate dreary introductions."

Seana saw in her a mind a brief vision of herself and Ari in bed and wondered if he had projected that to her on purpose. Then Otto said something that she didn't hear but as she looked at him she saw a flash of twin eagles on tall sculptured columns. Ari then started saying something as her attention came back to the table.

"—glad you met my mentor," Ari said.

"'My tor-mentor,' you're thinking," Otto said.

"Reading my mind," Ari said with a feigned chuckle.

"How are you his mentor?" Seana asked Otto diffidently.

Otto projected a false modesty.

"He and his associates gave me the resources to focus on one area—making money," Ari explained.

"And we got him to realize that his abilities are psychic," Otto said.

Ari nodded. "They taught me that those abilities are trainable—"

Concerned that he was saying too much already, Otto cut Ari off and offered Seana a crystal spoonful of caviar, talking continuously to distract her. "Have some Beluga, my dear. Yes, before we met him, Ari was an inventor—brilliant but poor, always getting ripped off, sucked down—but he still kept getting all these ideas! He had Idearrhea! Every day a new idea so glorious all the others were forgotten—"

Seana saw a vision of a younger Ari feverishly scribbling a note on a matchbook cover.

"Yes!" Otto went on, "You should have seen his files, Seana," he laughed. "Notes scrawled on matchbook covers, losing lottery tickets, corroded cheap hotel stationery—"

Seana had let slip words in her mind, which was against training. *Is he reading my mind?*

"We're all reading each other's minds!" Ari declared, "Isn't it fun?"

"Yes," Seana agreed nervously, and turned to ask Otto a question.

Otto saw it coming and intercepted it by offering her pâté and saying, "Here, my wicked little witch, you must try some of this wicked little Strasbourg."

Seana politely accepted and began to taste it, while Otto went swiftly on. "Well, tell me, how did you two happen to meet—" Seana's mouth was full.

"She arranged it," Ari stepped in.

"Ho, ho—how interesting." Otto laughed gaily. He nodded to Seana and she nodded back, chewing faster now, and trying to look innocent, as he went on, "I'll bet she wants to have your baby."

Ari laughed and Seana shook her head, gulping down the pâté.

Otto looked at Seana and had a vision of the front of the professional building where Theta was bivouacked. Seana picked up that something had just happened, that she had given something away, but she didn't know what it was. She looked briefly frightened and then instantly covered it with a blush and a smile.

"I think a relationship can be more torrid if there are *some* secrets..." she said, evoking a laugh from both of them.

"Well, Ari," Otto asked, "who do you think she's working for?"

Seana smiled casually, hiding her nervousness well, rising to the occasion at last.

Ari seemed to be providing a dramatic pause. "I think she was sent to us," he said after a beat or two.

"To do what with?" Otto asked.

"To be recruited," Ari said.

Seana started to say something but Otto interrupted, upset about Ari's openness.

"Sent by whom?" Otto demanded, suddenly taking charge.

"Well, by The Leaders of course," Ari said.

Otto looked irritated but instantly covered it.

Seana started to say something but Otto interrupted again.

"Are you so sure we can speak of these things in front of her, Ari?" Otto asked, with an edge in his voice.

"Well, of course," Ari said. Although he hadn't admitted it to himself, Ari was smitten with Seana. "My truth sense says I can trust her—that's got to be what you get—"

"Yes..." Otto said, turning to Seana. "Sorry, dear, but it's a heavy responsibility that's been placed on our shoulders... we know certain things that can't be talked about in front of most people."

"You two are just about the most fascinating pair of guys I've ever met," Seana said. "Who are The Leaders? What am I being recruited into? And are my psychic powers going to be trained—"

Ari laughed and said, "It's like a pressure to need to know in the loins of your mind, isn't it? Well, your excruciating pleasure of knowing will be even greater if we peel away the filmy undergarments over the truth, one at a time."

Otto had a brief vision of the three of them naked in bed together in a ménage à trois. Ari displayed a brief look of distaste and dropped it instantly. He made a small hand gesture and a three-piece band came out onto the terrace, set up, and began to play "Where or When". The music was well timed, almost muffling the noise of a gun battle that had erupted below. Waiters poured more champagne, cleared away the hors d'oeuvres, and delivered fresh plates of sushi and tapas.

Ari stood up and invited Seana to dance. He held her very close, rubbing his aroused genitalia against hers. "Now... is the time... of alignment," he whispered in rhythm with his rubs, his lips touching her ear.

Seana laughed, then recognized the phrase. "Of course! You heard the transmission too..."

"All *homo superiors* heard it," Otto said, as Ari began some serious dirty dancing with Seana.

Ω

Otto and Seana tangoed as Ari sat in with the band playing muted trumpet to the melancholy tune "Oh, These Dark Eyes". Otto looked deep into Seana's green eyes with their flecks of gold, seemingly entranced by her but actually trying to get more information without being caught at it again.

After his trumpet stint, Ari performed a complicated break-dance for their entertainment and to Seana's amazement, in a sort of male bird's mating dance. It had gotten dark and the colder air had started to make Seana tremble a bit, with her bare shoulders and back. Standing like a statue in a dark corner for most of the night, Cholmondeley saw Seana shiver, and at once went to fetch and bring her one of Ari's bulky cardigan Zegna sweaters, which she donned gratefully, hugging it to her body.

Then the band and the waiters and even the butler left the three of them alone, with occasional visits to refresh their glasses. They sat around the table, sipping their drinks, in a moment of sudden silence for the first time that evening.

"Ari," Seana asked, "what about the transmission? Who do you think sent it?"

"The Hidden Leaders," he said after a moment. "the fastest learners among Earth humans. The first to evolve beyond physical incarnation—"

Otto put on the brakes by jumping in with, "You may have heard them called the Ascended Masters." He shot a stern warning look at Ari, hoping Seana would not notice.

She looked at both of them. "You two seem pretty certain..."

Ari held up his glass to clink with them. "We're in touch with them," he bragged, and Otto winced as Ari ran on, "through our Magickal Order."

Seana turned to Otto, who felt embarrassed by Ari's boastful schoolboy behavior and how it reflected poorly on him. He made a faint facial gesture of assent.

"You mean you get transmissions like this all the time?" she asked.

They laughed. "Not so stepped up, of course," Otto allowed.

"Everyone gets transmissions sometimes," Ari added.

"Well, maybe not everyone," Otto said.

"So, which Magickal Order is that?" Seana asked.

"It's just called the Lodge," Otto quickly answered. He felt he had to take over the conversation from Ari, who would otherwise continue saying too much.

"Well, how come this particular transmission went out to non-members?" Seana asked.

"Six planets in a row pointed at Galactic Center," Ari said. "It's the signal for the start of a new age."

Otto jumped in again. "It's time to speed up evolution," he said.

She nodded.

"And you know what that means..." he went on, and she shook her head.

"A steeper challenge slope—faster learning by the superior ones, more of the inferior ones weeded out," he explained.

Seana looked unconvinced. "That's kind of an elitist thing to say, isn't it Otto?" she asked, and the two men laughed. "I mean the whole meaning of this transmission is that we are all one thing together. We can't dump the slow learners—" she insisted.

Otto cut in. "I don't want to do anything with the slow learners except leave them this classroom to... *hump* on, as they do, for a few million more lifetimes after I'm out of here."

"Otto just means he doesn't want them to slow us down," Ari explained.

"Sometimes those who could climb the ladder can't get on it because around its base crowd the unworthy, afraid to jump on themselves," Otto opined, vaguely paraphrasing someone.

Seana heard a helicopter whirring but paid it no mind, a few had flown by already tonight. She laughed at Otto's remark. "I don't know... I'd like to add a little humility in here: what if *we're* the slow learners?" she demurred.

"Then why are *we* getting the transmission?" Ari asked, and she had no answer. "See?" he said.

"I think I'm beginning to get... you think psychics are a new species," she started and saw their confirming looks. "Cro Magnons killed off the Neanderthals..." she trailed off.

"We're not planning on killing off all the *sapiens*," Otto said, "still less on them killing off all the *superiors*."

The helicopter sound had grown louder and closer. They all looked up and saw it coming toward them. Otto became agitated but relaxed as the copter swung sharply away.

"What's our talent for," Seana asked, "if not to protect the weak? If we use it against the weak—"

"As above, so below," Otto lectured. "There are parasites in the animal kingdom, therefore there are parasites at all levels—leeches, vampires, suckups—dragging you down—"

Ari interrupted him. "Seana's right, Otto, you need to have a bit more compassion for the Little People."

Otto unenthusiastically pretended to agree.

"Yes—those who have more have to give away more," Seana added.

"That's not what I said," Ari corrected her. "I said 'compassion' not 'giving'. The Universe is giving the slow learners exactly the kind of carrot-and-stick treatment they need to force them to evolve." He waited and she tentatively nodded agreement, then he went on. "Then social do-gooders like President Gomez come in and cushion the Universe's feedback with money taken away from the fast learners. Who does *that* help? That's not compassion," he concluded.

Seana was troubled but had no ready answer.

Otto looked proud of his pupil.

A little later, Seana indicated it was time for her to go home, saying she had to go to work in the morning. Ari joked, saying he thought she was a tarot card reader and she explained that she had a day job in market research, as in focus groups, working for a marketing research firm—which was Theta's cover in the professional building. The set up Theta rented had in fact been a focus group center, hence the one-way mirrored observer room.

When she stood up to leave, so did Ari and Otto. Ari stepped close to her and held her, kissing her for a full minute while Otto looked on with visible envy.

"You're sure you don't want Rex to drive you home?" Ari asked, still holding her close.

"No, really—I'd prefer to take a cab," she said, and noticed them both looking at her suspiciously. "I mean, in my neighborhood a stretch limo attracts too much attention." She turned and hugged Otto, and they saw her out. Ari had insisted she wear the sweater home in order not to catch cold.

Seana took a robocab back to the professional building. Like many in and near Manhattan, some floors of the building had been set up as apartments for corporate travelers and other temporary residents, and Theta had recently rented quite a few of those apartments, one of which was hers. She was eager to shower, feel clean again, and go to sleep with Marty in his room. But first, she'd need to write up at least a brief topline report.

She breezed into the reception area and the alarm went off.

Shannon, Williams, Khan, Page, and Donna flew into the room, guns ready to fire. Williams went to the wall screen and waved it on. It came up instantly, showing a silhouette picture of them shot from a ceiling corner. In Seana's silhouette something small glowed brightly.

"Not explosive," Williams said, "just a GPS."

"It's got to be in the sweater, she wasn't wearing it when she left," Shannon said. Wordlessly asking and being given permission to pat Seana down, he passed his hands over the sweater and pulled out what looked like a hatpin. "This is it."

Seana was stunned. "Damn. One of them planted a pin beacon on me."

"What's the other guy's name?" Shannon asked.

"Otto Wagner," Seana replied, as Donna tapped the name into her tablet. "How did you know about him?" Seana asked.

Shannon showed her a photo of the three of them at a table on Ari's roof terrace. "Remember a copter?"

"Donna, see what you can find out about Otto," he ordered, and then addressed the rest of them. "Who wants to take a nice long drive?"

"I'll go," Page volunteered, holding out his hand and receiving the pin beacon.

"If they're not too close behind, they might not notice that it stopped here," Shannon said optimistically. "Drive it out to Montauk and throw it in the ocean, then come home, go to sleep, and take the morning off."

Page quickly left and the alarm went silent.

Shannon, Seana, Williams and Khan grabbed coffee and went into a conference room to debrief Seana. Donna returned to her office to start her deep dive into the Otto character.

"I think Otto planted it on me," Seana said.

"You think Mann is on the level, legit?" Williams asked.

She shook her head in puzzlement as if she could not figure Ari out. "I've never seen anything like him. I guess he's a master—how he moves, everything he does, his timing—"

Williams could not help but notice that Seana's initial dislike of Ari Mann appeared to have taken a turn. He sensed a tinge of jealousy rising and immediately squelched it.

Seeing how Marty seemed to take in her comments about Ari, Seana then quickly added, "Sorry... I didn't mean to sound like a schoolgirl," which again caused him momentary pain which he again abnegated.

Shannon and Khan felt embarrassed to be in the room with these two lovers discussing "the other man". But they needed to debrief Seana while everything was sharp in her memory. Hence, they were still at it when Page got back hours later.

"Why aren't you sleeping?" Shannon asked Page as he entered.

"Got to know what Seana found out," Page said, still trying to figure himself out following the transmission. The experience of being Jesus had worn off a little and now he wondered whether it was true or not. Like most psychics he had always spent a lot of time exploring his own mind. Now, trying to discern his mission on Earth made him hungry for all the relevant information he could get.

"Mann and Wagner claim to be in cahoots with the sources of the transmission," Shannon said tiredly. He became sarcastic in his crankiness. "Super-hip humans evolved beyond bodies."

Page raised an eyebrow.

"They call them The Leaders—who, if they exist, would be considered a foreign power."

"Hence Wagner and Mann can be considered suspects of treason," Khan put in.

"Planting a bug isn't a friendly act..." Seana added.

Williams looked at her and then turned to Shannon. "If we're going to send Seana back there, we have to assume they know we found their bug. How do we protect her?" he asked.

Shannon strained, thinking fast, and feeling unsure. "She's got to come clean with Mann... tell him we want to recruit him—"

"But are we really recruiting him?" Williams asked.

"I don't know," Shannon admitted. "Maybe he's recruiting us... we need to know more about these so-called Leaders."

Ω

Wearing a gold silk dragon bathrobe, Ari was enjoying a soft boiled egg in his breakfast nook when his butler announced Otto, who no sooner stepped into the room. Ari did not rise to greet him.

"I see this popping in at odd hours has gotten to be quite a fetish with you, Otto," Ari said evenly.

"I live for it," Otto replied, sliding into the seat facing Ari and pouring himself some coffee. "I hate to tell you this, Ari, but our friend Seana is a spy."

"What?"

"She works for some branch of the U.S. government," Otto said.

"So? I pay my taxes. How do you know this, anyway?" Ari asked, going back to his egg.

"I took a picture of her," Otto said.

Ari looked querulous.

Otto pointed to one of the buttons on his double-breasted suit jacket, a different one from the other night. "This one's a camera, for example," Otto said.

Ari laughed.

"Yes, it's all a big joke," Otto said humorlessly. "She's on our Pentagon Face File."

"What's that?"

"We have a digitized record of every face that's entered the Pentagon, starting a few years back," Otto explained.

"Who's 'we'?" Ari asked, then realized it had to be The Leaders. "Oh, of course. So she's been in the Pentagon."

"Six days a week, starting earlier this year," Otto clarified, "until two weeks ago, when she popped up in *your* life—"

Ari's face darkened. "Too bad. I had really started to like her—what do they want with me?"

"Maybe they want to recruit you," Otto guessed.

Ari stared at him.

"They may be onto you as a psychic—not realizing your power comes through us—"

Ari hid his annoyance at Otto's supposition.

"I've got no interest in playing cloak and dagger games—don't worry, I'll get rid of her," he said conclusively.

"Not so easy. They seem to have found the bug I planted on her," Otto explained.

"The what? Otto, what is this nonsense with chairs, cameras, bugs—I'm an American citizen now—I don't want to get into trouble—I love this country."

"Don't worry, we're not being recorded right now—is your consciousness still so provincial?" Otto demanded. "Where's your highest allegiance? To the local fiefdom or to the Lords of Creation?"

Ari hid his distrust. "What do they want me to do?"

Otto looked satisfied. "If her people found the bug, she's going to come out of the closet and try to recruit you. Play hard to get—"

"That will be easy."

"—make them beg, but in the end, give in," Otto said, wrapping up.

Ari considered the proposition. "What's my motivation?" he asked.

"Curiosity."

"What's my real motivation?" Ari pressed.

"Our curiosity," Otto answered.

Ω

Ari and Seana rode around Central Park in the back of a horse-drawn hansom cab, giving each other a new rendition of reality. It was a beautiful day, marred only by the breach that had now come between them. Apparently incapable of forgiving, Ari acted coldly toward her. She felt thrown out of his heart, and for some reason it mattered to her, although she had never been romantically interested in him. But she wanted him as a friend because she found him interesting, and she was drawn to his good looks though he was too self-absorbed for her liking. Besides, Marty was her guy.

"It's okay," Ari said. "I just don't know if I can ever trust you again."

"I'm sorry, Ari."

"We're going to have to do this on my terms," Ari said. "I'm a good American. I haven't got time to be trained in your procedures. I'm going to train one of your team in my procedures. Then The Leaders will either link with your group or they won't. It won't be my problem anymore."

"Am I the one that you want to train?" she asked.

He looked at her. "I haven't got years," he said. Seeing that he had stung her deeply and felt good about it, he then felt bad. "I mean it isn't up to me—I want you and your people to pick your hero—the fastest learner, so I can return to my own life as soon as possible."

Ω

The Theta New York contingent gathered in the conference room: Shannon, Williams, Seana, Khan, Page, and Donna. Seana had given her report and now came the question of which one of them should go.

Page thought, *They're going to pick me.*

Shannon said, "You take this one Marty."

Page prayed silently, *Father! Forgive them!*

Shannon directed Williams, "Just stay off the nutty stuff, okay?" He went glassy-eyed and wobbled his head around in an idiot-like parody of the blissful Buddha face that Williams sometimes wore since hearing *The Message.*

To Seana and Williams he said, "Both of you, continue to play it his way as much as necessary until we know what the hell is going on."

Ω

Ari and Otto sat at a high-top, drinking single malt scotch at a trendy uptown bar. People, music, and noise formed a wall around them.

"We want him unconscious," Otto divulged.

Ari was incredulous.

"Otto, he's an officer of the U.S. Army—what are you trying to do to me—"

"Calm down. We *need* him unconscious. We have a desire to see what's in there," Otto said with a wry smile. "Any way you want to do it—Shannon agreed to 'no holds barred', remember? Use the *needle* or hit him over the head, bore him to sleep, I don't care—"

"Otto, you're exposing me to enormous danger. I'm not going to do it—"

"Ari, there's *no* danger. When he wakes up, he won't remember a thing we don't want him to remember. I promise you—we'll see to that."

"No," Ari said flatly.

Otto lit a cigarette, which was of course illegal inside any public space, and blew smoke. "Ari, have you looked at our contract lately?"

Their eyes met.

Ω

Ari was doing a yogic headstand in his exercise room when Cholmondeley showed Williams in. The butler bowed out and there was an elongated moment in which neither spoke.

Williams felt his mind being read. He left only certain parts visible. From his point of view, everything was of one piece, cellularized, and breathing. He saw himself and Ari as two parts of the same thing, engaging with itself.

Ari, still upside-down, his face set in hard lines, said, "Major Williams, I presume? Of America's illustrious—and secret—Theta Force. And now I see also the proud swain of Seana Moon."

"Good to meet you, too, Mr. Mann," Williams said affably, ignoring the demotion to major as he was now a light colonel.

"Theta waves... the most causative and elusive waves to psychics... so naturally it would be called Theta Force," Ari deduced.

"Actually," Williams said matter-of-factly, "Theta is next in the Greek alphabet after Delta." This was not true but it fooled Ari, who harrumphed, thinking himself proven wrong.

Williams felt compassion for everybody and was intuitively doing things to reduce Ari's ego for Ari's own sake. Williams had not been so inclusive in this strategy until he received *The Message*.

At the mention of Delta Force, Ari had picked up a momentary vision of a helicopter burning in the desert. He wondered about it briefly but cast it aside. He then got out of his upside-down position in one smooth move and stood facing Williams. He did not offer his hand.

"But really, the U.S. Army investigating psychic powers?" he asked Williams condescendingly.

"Since a failed rescue mission in Iran half a century ago, we've been investigating everything, including pacts with the Devil," Williams said, only half in jest.

Ari correctly connected his vision of the burning helicopter with the April 24, 1980 mission to which Williams had alluded. He had studied the tragedy in school and had seen the television news clips. A student of American history in both Russia and Israel, he had always wanted to be an American and now he was one. He had no intention of giving that up.

Williams sat down on a Nautilus bench without being invited to do so. "Speaking of the Devil, what's become of Otto Wagner?" he asked.

In a halting monotone, Ari replied, "He's gone away... I'm not going to talk about him... I'm going to teach you what I've been taught directly by The Leaders... it's my duty as an American citizen... but I want it to take as little time as possible... my co-investors and myself are losing millions of dollars because of this time I'm giving up tonight... so tonight is *it*."

"I understand—"

"If The Leaders won't pay attention to you when I'm finished with you, I wash my hands of you, too," Ari said.

For an instant, Ari saw a vision of himself going to shake hands with Williams, instead driving his fingers into Williams' solar plexus, Williams doubling over, Ari chopping him behind the ear. Reality returned as Williams spoke.

"I've already experienced a direct connection since the transmission... they've begun to speak to me," Williams shared.

"Good... although I don't see it in you now," Ari said.

Williams smiled and started to say something but Ari interrupted.

"Would you say I'm not being conducive to you being your highest self? Because I see your lowest self, which helps keep you there."

"Yeah," Williams agreed and would have continued but Ari interrupted again.

"Well, that's what each of us is doing to each other, every day. I am your guru. You have agreed to whatever methods I choose?"

Williams, standing up, replied, "I have."

Ari finally held out his hand and Williams moved to shake it. Ari moved with blinding speed to drive his hand into Williams' solar plexus, astounded a moment later to see that Williams had caught his hand and was now shaking it with gusto. He looked up to see Williams' smiling face and couldn't tell whether Williams was a lucky fool who thought that Ari was going to shake his hand, or if Williams had expected Ari's attack and was now playing Ari.

"Put 'er there, podner," Williams said in a cowboy-like twang.

Ari disengaged his hand. "Come... let's go to my office," he said.

"Sure," Williams agreed.

Ari ushered Williams ahead of him down the long dark corridor lined with art and statuary. "All the way to the end."

Walking behind Williams, Ari mentally saw himself chopping Williams behind the ear and Williams crumpling. Williams' back loomed closer as Ari started catching up to him.

Come on! He'll never know what hit him! Ari thought he heard Otto say that in his mind, but he wasn't sure he wasn't imagining it.

He briefly envisioned going to chop Williams, then Williams simultaneously turning to look at a piece of statuary, Ari striking the wall, Williams looking back at him with a mild almost neutral expression, Ari removing his hand from the wall to reveal a splattered cockroach. Then reality returned to Ari.

"You've got some really beautiful stuff in here," Williams said over his shoulder.

Williams preceded Ari into Ari's electronic office. Acronyms and prices still marched across a couple of the screens.

"Have a seat," Ari said, indicating the Gothic chair, as he himself sat at his desk.

Williams sat on the needle chair, asking, "What is this, your Inquisition chair? Doesn't fit the rest of your office."

"I got it just for you," Ari said, "so I could make you feel really comfortable."

Williams tried to see if he could get it to recline, which he could not. "Hmm.... not a Barcalounger..." he muttered.

"Sorry," Ari said, and looked at his watch. "Now, Major, I think I can go through this rather quickly if you don't interrupt."

Williams nodded.

"I don't want you to be able to accuse me of not giving you what you came for, nor to have an excuse to try to bother me again."

Williams shook his head. "Of course not."

"Here it is," he said, leaning forward and putting his hands on the desk. "You want to contact The Leaders, those who have evolved farthest in their incarnations here on Earth. You must become empty—internally free of all attachments. Willing to lose everything. Not caring if you die—not hanging on to any pet beliefs, or image of yourself; totally open. Beyond the illusion. You have to give up this plane." One of his hands moved casually on the desk edge, bringing his thumb near the button. "Freedom is the highest quality. It attracts Them to you—but you can't fake it. You have to be really free. Enlightened—"

"Why is freedom the highest?" Williams asked.

Ari was irritated by the interruption. "Because we are given responsibility only for ourselves... it's our duty to do the most we can with our own potential."

His thumb felt around for the button.

"Wait a second," Williams objected calmly. "The essence of the transmission is that we are all one thing. How does that jibe with maximizing our own selfish freedom?"

Ari's irritation mounted with each interruption, further exacerbated because his thumb couldn't find the button.

"The essence of the transmission is stepped-up power. There is no message beyond that," Ari said, based on his own experience.

Williams responded incredulously. "What? We all got a message—"

"That all happened in your own heads. It's just stepped-up power."

His thumb found the button and rested upon it, ready to go. He felt a wave of relief but hoped it didn't show.

"Come on—we all got the same message. Maybe it didn't come from your Leaders but from somebody else...?"

"Like whom?" Ari smiled sarcastically. "God, perhaps?"

"Perhaps," Williams allowed. He himself felt sure of it.

"You hopeless primitive!" Ari said, raising his voice. "You can barely get your mind around the concept of one God. You're still light years away from being able to accept the Truth: in the beginning was Elohim..."

"What does that mean?" Williams asked.

"Elohim is plural. There is no one God. Each of us is a god. Some of the other gods have tried to fool us into becoming their slaves." His thumb started to press down on the button.

Williams leaped up and paced the floor. "Oh no, I'm sure you are not right about that. I don't get it—how do The Leaders and the transmission fit together if it didn't come from them?"

Ari blew up. "You're sure *I'm* not right? I thought *you* came here to get instruction from *me*—"

He noticed the needle sticking up visibly out of the chair and jumped to his feet. "Let's go next door, I need a drink!"

He bustled Williams toward a door on the opposite wall, opened it, and stood back to let Williams go through. Then he kicked Williams powerfully in the butt, propelling him into the next room.

Williams rolled head over heels down the steps into Ari's sunken living room, knocking over a large statue and lamp which smashed through a glass armoire filled with crystal and other *objets d'art*. Ari dove onto him and they rolled over and over, smashing a Lalique clear crystal coffee table. Williams rolled free. They came up circling. Ari attacked and Williams deflected his kicks and blows without striking back, as they proceeded to destroy the rest of the fabulously expensive contents of the room.

Ari stopped for a moment, out of breath. "Fight back, you bastard!" he yelled.

Williams, also out of breath, responded evenly, "Haven't wanted to... hurt anybody lately."

Ari snickered. "Great quality in a soldier! What kind of protection are you for the Free World?"

Williams continued to see everything in the room as one piece, cellularized and breathing. Ari attacked him and Williams threw him back. Ari grunted as he crashed painfully into furniture. Williams grunted too, realizing he felt Ari's pain with him.

Ari leaned on a wall, catching his breath. "Pretty good for an old man," he said, although Williams was only a few years older than Ari.

"I wasn't this good last week... before *The Message*... now that I trust, it does itself; I just watch," Williams said, though still breathing hard.

This was true. Williams had been surprised by his keen fighting abilities, which had never been at that level before.

Ari's eyes slitted. "You know they gave me a license to kill you. Absolving me in the case of any accident. Your friend Colonel Shannon signed it. Did you know that?"

"Yes. It's Standard Operating Procedure."

"Even Seana was in favor. She said they'd leave me alone if you accidentally didn't come back from the initiation that I gave you—and she said you'd be out of our way then," Ari lied, attempting to weaken Williams' defenses.

Suddenly Ari threw a vase at Williams. As Williams ducked, Ari landed a kick in his face, and then followed up with other kicks and blows until Williams regained his defensive stance, his face bloodied now.

"Don't worry," Ari said, "if you die, I'll let you sit in my mind sometimes when I do it to her."

"You're a prince," Williams said.

Again Ari attacked and again Williams threw him back. As Ari flew across the room, the large solid-looking oak door flew open and Ari's head cracked into it, knocking him out cold on the floor.

The butler entered wide-eyed. "I heard noise, sir—" Cholmondeley said in a panicky voice, rushing to kneel by his master, dabbing away blood from Ari's forehead with his formerly immaculate handkerchief.

"We were sparring but now you appear to have hurt him when you opened that door," Williams said in a consoling voice, though at the same time wanting to make it perfectly clear what had happened. He went to check the pulse in Ari's throat.

"But sir! The room—your face—" the butler said, dumbfounded at the implausible situation.

"Just having a little fun," Williams deadpanned.

Ari's pulse was strong. "Good... he'll be okay," Williams assured Cholmondeley confidently, and headed for the door, adding over his shoulder, "I think I've got as much information as I could here—please tell Mr. Mann I won't be bothering him again. Good night."

"Good night, sir," the butler said haplessly.

Down in the street, Williams sensed people in all directions looking at him as if he ought to be hospitalized immediately. A cellular bubble encased everything, and everything inside the bubble—the skyscrapers, the bustling people, the cars—everything was attached to the insides of the bubble, including himself, as he moved along the street swiftly. He hailed the first robocab he saw and got in and gave the address. Then he used the few tissues he had to clean up his appearance a bit. He took out his tablet and started on some research.

When he walked into home base, his team—overtaken with concern—wordlessly ministered to his wounds at once. He had walked away with only surface wounds, which would heal in time with the advanced medicines the team applied.

Finally they went to the conference room and sat down. Williams chose the seat by the main white board.

"Okay, let's hear it," Shannon said.

"He kicked me in the butt to start the fight, then told me how Seana encouraged him to kill me, then he did his best to do so," Williams explained, smiling at Seana.

She went white for a second then saw that Marty was kidding her, perhaps exaggerating an innuendo.

"Why did he want to kill you?" Shannon asked coolly.

"Seana," Williams said. "He's quite taken with her and thinks it's two-way."

"Good," Shannon said quickly before anyone else could speak. That's what they wanted him to think. Otherwise Seana would not be able to get any more information out of him. "What else did you learn?"

"He got no message in the transmission. He said it was just about stepped-up power, that's all."

Everyone shook their heads in disbelief. Digital magazine and television news reports from thousands of psychics all over the Internet relayed variations on the same message. Including the top psychic in the world, the Danang Lama.

"How can Ari, who is such a powerful psychic himself, not have heard *The Message*?" Seana wondered.

"I think it has something to do with the philosophy he was taught," Williams guessed.

"Taught by whom?" Shannon asked quickly.

"By Otto and whomever he represents," Seana responded for Williams, who nodded.

"How could some philosophy keep a psychic from hearing a message that most other psychics heard?" Shannon mused out loud, feeling lame.

"*The Message* about all of us being one thing—the connectedness that I'm now experiencing directly—is the opposite of what Ari learned from the people who took him off the streets, bankrolled him and focused him," Williams revealed.

"So Ari couldn't let it in—" Seana got it.

"Marty," Shannon said, switching the focus off of Ari. "Tell us about this connectedness you're experiencing." From his tone it seemed as if he felt concern about Williams' mental state. That became his top priority.

"I see everything that way now. And when Ari jumped me, my body just took over, I was just a passenger," Williams said. "I had never fought that well before, even in my prime in the bush."

"So then, this connectedness might be a good thing—we could all benefit from it," Shannon said, as if laying out a hypothesis.

Listening until now, Khan spoke up. "We know what it is, Tim. It's the Zone, Flow state—we've known about that for years."

"Good God, man, you're right!" Shannon got it. "Williams, you're able to sustain that level over time now—?"

"Apparently," Williams answered modestly.

"Well, that will help," Shannon said, with some relief from his earlier concern. He began to see the odds shift from impossible to possible. "Tell me more about this philosophy Otto's people taught him."

Seana jumped in. "Otto and Ari made it real clear that they oppose the president because he is allocating too much resource to bad breeding stock. Their preference is for Social Darwinism—survival of the fittest carried to a fascist extreme. That's my takeaway."

Williams nodded agreement. "That and fanatical desire for individual selfish freedom and independence, the opposite of Oneness," he added.

"So who are Otto's people?" Shannon asked.

"Some fascist group," Jason threw out. He had been quietly thinking of how to reveal his divinity and be accepted for who he really was. There had to be a way and he would find it. It was his duty. Now he was trying to be the one who helped them get focused.

"Yes," Williams agreed. "It's possible the president didn't just act on personal interest in assigning us to Ari. There is something going on, behind Ari, and it's on us to get to the root of it."

"An organized fascist underground led by psychics..." Shannon mused. "That doesn't sound very pleasant."

He thought for a moment. To his understanding, fascists generally knew the value of weapons and tended to have a lot of them. And they threw away the rules along with conventional fair play.

"If this is something that's had time to grow, its proportions could be far greater than we might imagine..."

"How are we going to go about getting any closer to Ari?" Jason asked Shannon, who looked up at him patiently despite Jason's seeming impertinence.

"Any ideas?" Shannon asked authentically.

An idea popped into Jason's head as if from God. "Yes, actually," Jason said. "What if I approach him through the Martial Arts Association to challenge him to a blindfold bout? He won't know I'm with you guys."

"That *is* a good idea," Shannon said.

"Seana, you said you met Ari's instructor," he said and she nodded.

"Why don't Jason and Khan challenge Ari and his instructor to a blindfold bout for charity," Shannon suggested.

Jason looked momentarily deflated then cheered back up and traded glances with Khan, and they both smiled, nodding enthusiastically.

Ω

At first Ari was cold to the idea. He had never fought wearing a blindfold, and he did not want to lose in public, it would break his perfect record.

Recovering from the bash in the head by the next morning, Ari was back to normal. Cholmondeley found this astonishing, though gave it no further thought as he had his hands full cleaning up the living room and ordering replacement furniture.

Ari had not apprised Otto of the blindfold challenge so was annoyed but not surprised when Otto announced that he knew about it. Otto began to push him to accept the duel but Ari held firm against being influenced.

Otto was going to bring up the contract again, when he suddenly hatched an alternate plan. A gleeful look came over his face. Reporting to the Top, he set the plan in motion.

Relaxing in his Jacuzzi and listening for stock tips and other even more important suggestions from The Leaders, Ari felt the voice of what he thought of as God speaking to him. He paid rapt attention, and heard, *"I will win the fight for you."*

This focused his mind as never before. Did he fully trust The Leaders? Surely this was a test they had set up for him. If he didn't fight, they would know he didn't fully trust them, and then what might happen? He decided he had to fight. He would do it on one condition: before the blindfold bout, they would do a warm-up spar without blindfolds so that the audience would know how good he is when not blindfolded.

Conditions accepted, arrangements made, the date came quickly. The bout was to be televised live by stream and on a global cable/satellite network, with ads and sponsor contributions to New York's homeless to be distributed by the Guardian Angels.

Backstage in the green room, the combatants met for the first time and shook hands all around. "Good to meet you." "Pleasure." Ari gave Khan a passing glance, instantly assessing him to be a pushover at his age, and then studied Jason with focused attention. Each of them studied their opponents with the same single-pointed attention.

"After this I hope we can take you out to dinner," Jason offered.

Ari, about to refuse, heard himself agree. *My body is starting to take over,* he told himself. *Well I had better not resist that!*

Great cheering arose from the prompted studio audience as the warriors came on camera. The host announced them and soon the crowd noise died down.

The men began circling. This was the warm-up sparring, with eyesight. As expected, Ari made the first aggressive move, a feint toward Khan then a kick aimed at Jason's kneecap, which would have exploded except that Jason got out of the way in time. The other fighters' eyes widened at Ari's move. "Sparring" like that is simply not done in martial arts.

"Sorry," Ari said hollowly, and then launched a different attack on Khan, which Khan parried. The fight became fully engaged with all four men fighting at once. The two teams appeared perfectly and evenly matched—very few shots got through. After the clock ran out, and following a brief respite for commercials, the audience oohed and ahhed expectantly as the blindfolds were put on. Khan and Jason had also fought each other with their ears plugged but that wasn't a feature of tonight's duel.

Khan and Jason quickly showed their dominance in the blindfold bout. They did not hurt Ari or his instructor but could not help but embarrass them. As the television time had to be filled, the bout went on. But now something different happened: Khan and Jason, following each other's hunches, began to make a little sound—heavy breathing, occasional small grunts—to give away their positions, allowing the other two men to get in some blows and kicks. The audience went wild when they saw that their heroes had come back from behind, showing themselves to be superfast learners. They were going to win after all!

This of course had always been Theta's plan.

The audience went wild at the stunning climax, when Jason purposely got knocked down. Tearing off their blindfolds, Ari and his instructor offered their hands to help Jason to his feet, and then slapped each other on the back, laughing together about what great fun the fight had been.

The buoyant mood carried them into the lavish dinner at a French place near the studio, which Ari had picked, insisting dinner was on him. His instructor had to bow out to get home to his ailing wife.

Over drinks, Ari sought to learn as much as he could about these men, thinking there might be a place for them in his life. Perhaps The Leaders had sent them. Perhaps they were even of The Leaders.

They fed him the covers they had been given, which were mostly true and would stand up to investigation. Khan really did own a Chinese restaurant in Manhattan, which also housed a Taoist temple at which he presided on certain days. And Jason really did star in extreme fighting shows on television.

"How did you guys meet?" Ari asked over the first course.

"We met in a steel cage on a TV show," Khan said with a smile.

"Khan had been doing blindfold since he was four years old," Jason said, smiling fondly at Khan. "And I got interested in it and sought him out to teach me. Then, when he said I was ready, we did some cage fighting against each other. It was very lucrative and seemed to put ladies into a sporty mood."

The men laughed a male locker-room kind of laugh. The Theta agents had achieved their desired result, having played the scene as a bonding ritual.

Jason was going with the Flow and the fact that he saw himself as Jesus wasn't dazzling his ego at the moment. He was staying in the moment and would come back to his mission as Jesus some other time. His Theta training had kicked in.

The second course had arrived, and Ari now had to ask, "Is there some other reason you gentlemen sought me out?"

"Of course, everybody wants to meet you," Jason admitted, and Khan nodded, smiling.

"Why is that, do you suppose?" Ari asked with an amused smile.

"You and the Danang Lama," Jason said, "the most evolved human beings on the planet." Ari touched his immaculate napkin to his lips and nodded immodestly.

"You weren't hatching some investment scheme, by any chance?" Ari asked, still smiling.

The two laughed and so did Ari.

"Of course—heh-heh—if you would like us to hatch one, we're at your service," Khan jested.

The way Ari's mind worked, it took less than a second to concoct an idea. "Okay, I see it. Here is how it will work. We open up a chain of fight training schools across the country and call it The Mann School. We advertise plus we have our own show. The students get to do blindfold duels on television and streaming. You guys do all the work, I bankroll it, and make appearances now and then."

Khan and Jason looked at each other in awe and looked back at Ari. "What a great idea, boss!" Jason said, and Khan smiled, nodding.

"You got me with the sporty ladies," Ari revealed.

Ω

Shannon did not think it was such a great idea. "I think we just got sucked into recruiting and training the fascist army," he opined.

They were sitting in the conference room. Jason got it and was rocked back. "You're right..." he admitted reluctantly, and Khan hung his head in shame.

"Well, don't worry, we'll make the most of it," Shannon encouraged them. "You had to accept Ari's offer or the trail would have gone cold right there. The whole fight sham would have been a waste of time."

"Maybe we can slow roll it," Jason added.

But none of them anticipated the speed with which Ari Mann could or would carry out his ideas. The fight schools were in the media the next day. Ari liked to launch things overnight—it was fun.

Jason and Khan got to see Ari every night in the fight clubs, where Ari got to meet the purported sporty women. These included clubs they didn't own yet—Ari was deciding which ones to buy. The current owners had already picked up on this, thinking about whether to start the conversation with Ari or wait for him to make the first move.

That first week, Ari was reclining backward in his tux on the semi-clad body of a sporty and very young woman who had just been seduced by seeing him win a no-holds-barred fight in a steel cage. Jason saw the moment as his opportunity to escalate. This had all been discussed in advance. Khan gave him the eye signal confirming he agreed.

"Ari," Jason said smiling, Ari beaming back, "we are from The Leaders."

Ari's smile vanished, then came cautiously back. "I thought that might be the case," he said, looking intently at the two of them. "I've been waiting for you to say something. But is this the right time—?" he asked, signaling with his eyes that he meant the girl. She looked up.

"She's with us," Jason said, and Donna shook Ari's hand and met his eyes.

Ari now realized he would probably not get to be in bed with her tonight but he showed nothing. He now treated them deferentially, as would be appropriate, while inside he held a degree of skepticism.

"You must know Otto, who has always been our go-between—?" Ari asked casually, smiling.

The three smiled back. "We know him, but he doesn't know us," Khan said. "He's a rogue—a Rebel—"

"He's on the other team," Jason added.

"There are two teams of Leaders?" Ari asked, his eyebrows rising. He looked around, now on edge.

"The Leaders and a split-off faction," Donna clarified. She knew their team had to be positioned as the legitimate one. They had drilled on their storyline for days.

"What caused the split?" Ari asked, now genuinely interested whether the story was true or not.

"One personality rebelled and persuaded the others to follow," Jason said.

He had the sudden feeling he remembered having been there. *But this is just a made-up story Theta concocted to position us as more "Leaders" than Otto,* he told himself.

None of the agents had any idea that their made-up story was also true. The ideas were leaking through from their asleep souls into their brains—no one realized these were memories from other lives.

"Who is this rebel?" Ari asked.

"We remember him as Lucifer," Donna replied. "He has many names."

Ari suddenly saw the connection between Judaism and The Leaders. "And so who is the head of your team?"

"The One Self," Khan said, "the Tao in my lingo. The same self that is in each of us, and in everything."

"So... even Lucifer... and his rebels... are really The One Self, but don't know it?" Ari asked, trying to wrap his mind around the concept.

"They don't want to know it," Jason said. "You know Otto and I don't, but I suspect you may have noticed some aberrations in him—?" he ventured.

"Well, yes," Ari admitted.

"These rebels and their leader have gone a bit mad," Donna attested.

"They call themselves The Leaders but they aren't qualified to lead," Jason put in.

"You'll be able to decide for yourself over time which of us are the more plausible true Leaders," Khan said with authenticity.

Ari's mind began to open, though he realized he would have to play both sides until he really knew for sure which one was genuine—or if they both were, which side he should join. His repugnance for Otto biased him but he knew he'd have to ignore his own biases to choose the right side. He suddenly felt afraid, caught up in something far larger than himself, something he could not control. The wrong move could get him killed.

The next morning he instructed Cholmondeley: "Hire the six toughest bodyguards in the world—they have to be former Navy SEALS or the like and still in violent occupations—pay any price they ask. Have them each get here as fast as possible. Get the three closest available apartments in the building or within a block. And get the guest rooms ready to always have three of them here."

The butler stared at him, suddenly afraid, and said, "Yes, sir."

Ω

Seana noticed the difference in Marty in bed. *He really is in the Flow state all the time,* she thought to herself.

He noticed that she seemed melted by his presence. She crooned more than ever before, sounding like the most beautiful music he had ever heard.

In their orgasm together, he saw her as she looked in many other lives, and she saw him as he looked in those lives. In the warm afterglow, they spoke.

"You've always been my teacher, as you are now," she whispered.

"Yes, your real name is Layla," Williams revealed from what he had just experienced. "It's what we've always called you."

"Who is this 'we'—?"

"We're a team—there are five of us, I think," Williams said.

"What is our mission?"

"I have no idea," Williams confessed.

"Whom do we work for?" she asked.

"The One Self, as in the story we gave Ari." It had begun to dawn on him. "It wasn't just a story..." he trailed off, dazed by the enormity of what felt like a revelation.

"Are you going to tell Shannon?" Seana asked, wide-eyed, sensing the reality of the story.

"He already thinks I'm crazy," Williams replied. "I want to tell him right now but it will be better to wait for the right time."

10

A New York-sized crowd, punctuated by saffron-clad Buddhists and Hindus, clogged First Avenue in midtown Manhattan, swarming around cars and limousines arriving at the United Nations. Shannon got out of a robocab and hustled through the crowd to the security booth outside the Delegates' Entrance.

A very tall man stood outside the booth and smiled broadly at Shannon, who did the same back. They hugged.

"Jeez, Pete, it's good to see you," Shannon said warmly.

"Been a long time, Tim—some reunion at the Point—six, seven years ago?" Pete said.

"Maybe," Shannon replied.

"You're into this psychic stuff in a serious way, now, right?" Pete asked.

"Stuff really works," Shannon said softly, "half the time." They both laughed. "So, what's the scoop on the last minute change?"

Pete escorted Shannon past the guard booth, nodding at the guard who signaled deferentially, through the line of limos, and on to the Delegate's Entrance.

"It got switched from the General Assembly to the Delegate's Lounge—I guess you know that already," Pete said, and Shannon nodded. "They're only letting in psychics with credentials to the lounge. The address will be going out on world television and streaming—there's a giant screen in the General Assembly so the other delegates can watch it—"

"I don't get it," Shannon admitted.

"Maybe he prefers to stand in front of an audience he knows is unarmed," Pete reasoned. "The Danang Lama's live audience today—except you—is coming in through the metal detectors at the public entrance. And then those that pass credentials screening get into the lounge where they can see him live."

"What, did he have a premonition or something?" Shannon joked.

"That's what the rumors say," Pete said. "Hey! Maybe you *are* psychic!" They grinned ironically at each other.

The United Nations Delegates Lounge is an enormous long room with a high vaulted ceiling, a long wall of windows, a mural of the Great Wall of China on the other long wall, and stairs going up to a mezzanine at the back of the room. Normally filled with couches and coffee tables, today rows of folding chairs faced the podium at the front of the room. Large rollaway fabric screens created a backdrop behind the podium. Three TV cameras stood ready, pointed at the podium.

The global, exotic-looking crowd of psychics filed in through the entrance doors to the left of the podium, wearing many odd clothes, hats, and expressions. All eyes seemed to gaze back searchingly into their own.

In their midst was Otto Wagner, wearing enormous wraparound sunglasses, which made him look odd and so made him fit in. Otherwise, with his impeccable suit, he would have seemed out of place. Looking around, he recognized no one until he saw Ari Mann come in. He signaled Ari to join him in the second row center.

"Otto, you're not serious about that disguise?" Ari asked, sitting down beside Otto.

"What dis—oh, the glasses. No disguise. Horrible eye infection. Spoils my perfect features," Otto reported.

Ari tried to see around the side of the glasses but couldn't see Otto's eyes.

Otto went on in a lower voice, looking straight ahead at the podium, "The Leaders consider you a bungler and now it's reflecting badly on me."

"It was an accident," Ari objected. "If Chumley hadn't barged in—"

"There are no accidents," Otto said scathingly. "He won because he projected helpful intervention and he got it. You were still fighting on the material plane despite your training."

"How do *you* know?" Ari challenged, and they stared icily at each other, as if considering pitched battle.

Seana came into the lounge area and saw them but they didn't notice her. She hesitated and Shannon came up from behind and guided her to their seats.

"Wait until after this ends," he counseled. "Leave with Mann, if possible, and find out his side of what happened with Marty."

"You don't trust Marty any more—" she blurted.

"Sounds like maybe *you* don't—" Shannon shot back softly. "I just want to know why Ari risked our reprisal by beating Marty up—release form or no release form. When this is over, stay with him..."

Seana had a brief flash of seeing herself in bed with Ari later.

Williams found seats toward the rear as the Lounge had filled up quickly—many were resigned to standing in the back and along the sides of the hall. Arriving separately—as if by accident already sitting in the adjacent seats and pretending not to know him—Donna, Khan and Jason needed to keep up their cover in case Ari turned around and looked back.

Williams heard in his mind the wordless murmuring of many voices, out of which one intelligible female voice emerged, with a New York accent: *Is everybody listening?*

The lights dimmed slightly. Guards appeared at the entrance and began turning people away, redirecting them to the General Assembly hall. One person continued to bull her way in—a very beautiful curvaceous young woman of mixed race—Nastassia Slayevsky, just arrived from Russia.

Jason saw her from across the large room and his heart skipped a beat. She was unaware of him as she made her way past the guards, walking quickly to the back where she found a spot to stand against the wall. Jason started to stand but Williams restrained him with a word, "Later."

"It's... the woman in the window," he whispered to Williams, Donna, and Khan.

"She would be here, now wouldn't she," Williams whispered back. "Well, how great for you! Just wait for this thing to be over before you go after her, okay?"

Jason nodded reluctantly.

"Find out who she is without giving out any real information," Williams added, still speaking in a hushed tone.

Jason looked confused but again nodded, this time grudgingly.

The lights on the podium brightened and the cameras' red lights came on. An offstage male voice announced in an Oxford-British accent, "Ladies and gentlemen, the Danang Lama." There was instant rousing applause, with many standing and smiling, hooting, whistling, and expressing love.

The Danang Lama stepped out between fabric screens and up to the podium, smiling radiantly. Great-grandson of a South Vietnamese war hero, a psychic preacher of peace discovered by global media, he was a teenager with a strong presence, uncanny wisdom, and unerring foresight. On television he proved over and over again his ability to read minds.

The way he sensed the world was like the way Williams sensed the world, except that in addition to the all-of-one-piece, cellular view, the Danang Lama also saw each person as luminous.

The Lama held up his arms to silence the applause and people sat down, all ears, some of them also attempting mind contact with him.

"Thank you all for coming," the Lama said. "We've had this date for quite some time now." A few people got the double entendre and laughed. He was referring to the planetary alignment.

Although at some distance apart, the Danang Lama and Williams made eye contact.

"Some hear one stream of inspiration," the Lama said matter-of-factly, "One initiate hears all those streams... that is me."

The Danang Lama made eye contact with Nastassia. "Where is Templegard?" he asked, and the rest of the audience wondered what that meant. So did Nastassia. Shannon saw that the Lama was not looking at him, so he knew someone else in the audience must know Templegard too, if it was the same Templegard—but how many people have that name? So it must be the same one. How would the Lama know about Templegard? Did he really know about everybody? And to whom was he speaking...?

The Lama then made eye contact with Shannon, and Seana, and Khan, and Page, and Donna, and then Ari. "So many familiar faces... happy to see you..." he said.

He saw Otto and added "Some of you..." with a gentle smile. "Well, it's always fun to dance with you all, no matter how you dance the dance."

He turned a bit more serious. "We're here to discuss *The Message*. The cosmic clock triggered this event, signaled last week by the lineup of six planets—Saturn, Jupiter, Mars, Venus, Mercury, and Earth—pointing at the center of the Milky Way. It's evolution time!"

He looked briefly at Otto. "When this evolution starts to happen through you... don't become arrogant and think that it makes you better than anyone else... it will come to everyone eventually."

In his luminous connected vision the Lama saw a little Black girl in the front row offering him a rose. He smiled at her.

"Those getting the talents sooner should help the others get them—" he went on.

The little girl stood up and held out the rose.

"And when you too start hearing voices in your head, remember that you can't believe all you hear. It's your responsibility to discriminate before fully accepting channeled information, because there are not one, but—" he paused to briefly

step over to receive the proffered rose and kiss the little girl on
her forehead.

At the same instant, a shot went off and pandemonium
erupted. The shot, intended for the Lama but missing him as he
moved to get the rose, was a plastic explosive bullet launched
from Otto's sunglasses, which blew up against the metal frame
of one of the rollaway screens, causing a very loud blast sound.
With redoubled fear, some people in the sea of bodies surging
to get out fell down. Theta agents quickly stepped in, restoring
order in their vicinity, and helping people up who might have
otherwise been trampled to death. Some were still screaming.

Ari, as dazed as most, hadn't taken note of Otto's reaction
to whatever was going on. By the time he looked over, Otto had
left. He looked around quickly and saw Otto moving away from
the entrance and toward the back of the room. Ari figured Otto
knew another way out and so followed him, against the flow of
the crowd.

Flailing arms knocked off Otto's sunglasses and he let them
go, proceeding toward his escape route. He of course had no
eye infection. Looking backward, he saw Seana following him,
and behind her, Ari. He tried to move faster.

Williams had reached the podium to find and protect the
Danang Lama but he was nowhere in sight. On the floor near
where the fabric screens parted, he saw the luminous rose. He
stepped through the part between the screens.

As Seana neared Otto, he swung around with perfect timing to deliver an edge-of-the-hand blow to the side of her neck,
pretending it to be accidental. Stunned, she fell to the floor,
where the crowd began to trample over her. By the time Ari
reached her and lifted her up, she was only half conscious. He
half-carried, half-walked her out the main entrance, turning to
see Otto disappearing up the stairs to the mezzanine.

Still in the Diplomats Lounge, Shannon had retrieved
the deadly eyeglasses, which he held by the tip of one temple. Knowledge of exactly what had happened had just come
together in his mind, as if given to him by someone else.
Thanks, he thought.

Our pleasure, he heard.

God? No answer, but a fond chuckle. Sounded like a friend he once had but he couldn't place it exactly. Maybe Afghanistan...

Templegard, half a world away from the UN event, in fact had also received *The Message* and had been changed by it, but in a much subtler way. A block had been placed by an ancient enemy in his mind that made him extremely skeptical of psychic powers. He didn't know he had received *The Message* but it had changed his dreams. Now, in his dreams every night, he dreamed of the team on the spacecraft, his buddies—where they were now and what he could do to help them. These felt like just good dreams to him. But in them, he was also picking up and giving clues to his teammates.

Shannon was the only teammate who knew Templegard in this life, and he had no idea that he was receiving tips from him in dreams. Neither of them knew this was going on.

Ω

Fully awake now, Seana's neck really hurt. Ari gently rubbed it with his right hand while with his left hand, in typical show-off style, he operated the manual gear shift of his classic-red Ferrari F60 America convertible, maneuvering precariously through hypercompetitive Manhattan truck and taxi and car traffic.

"Oh, no, Otto's a perfect gentleman, he would never do anything like that. You just got hit by someone's flailing arm—"

"I guess ... you probably saved my life," she said weakly.

Ari got suddenly outraged by a thought. "They shot at the Danang Lama when he started to say, 'There are not one, but multiple Gods'!"

"Is that what he was starting to say?" she asked with a touch of skepticism.

"Of course!" Ari insisted. "You know who shot at him? It was your friend Williams!"

Seana laughed softly. "Marty? He'd never do anything like that." She looked at him. "What have you got against Marty anyway? Why'd you beat him up?"

Ari feigned surprise. "Didn't he tell you? He swung at me when I said there was no one God."

"He didn't tell it that way," Seana said guardedly.

"He probably didn't remember," Ari said, looking over at her and back at the road repeatedly. "I tried to get him in touch with the real source of the transmission but Williams seems to have his own agenda—a false single God that doesn't exist. You guys will go on endlessly making up your own realities while Lamas get shot and The Leaders ignore you. Maybe *you* should have been the one I taught..."

He turned back to look at the road just in time to smoothly avoid a collision, downshifting with his left hand to accelerate again.

"Give me the chance now," Seana submitted.

Ari thought it over. "Okay," he said.

"I just need to get clearance," she said, somewhat surprised.

He bristled. "Now or never," he said.

Tim, I need clearance now, she sent telepathically and hoped Tim would get it.

Stay with him, she heard Tim say in her mind. Or did she just remember him having said that?

A moment later, she surrendered to Ari. "Okay."

"My rules... you do whatever I say," he stipulated.

"Right," she acceded.

He inched along the clogged crosstown streets from the East River to upper Park Avenue and she closed her eyes, later realizing she had slept a little. Still feeling tired and weak when they arrived at Ari's building, he carried her to his personal elevator as the doorman parked the Ferrari. Entering his penthouse, he dismissed the butler for the night and carried Seana into his bedroom.

She awoke alone on the bed, still dressed, her shoes off, rubbing her neck. Turning her head painfully to the left, she noticed a one-piece coverall lying over a chair. She recognized it as the outfit Mann wore on their first date—dress shoes, socks, suit, shirt, and tie, all one piece for stepping into and zipping up, the zipper covered by a placket.

Mann appeared carrying a tray with a glass of water and a pill, set it down and sat on the bed.

"So, that's how you got dressed so fast," she muttered, indicating the coverall.

"One of my early inventions," Ari said.

"Everything about you isn't an illusion, is it?" Seana asked, her voice still sleepy.

"Not everything," he answered drily. "Here, take this," he said, offering the pill and the water.

"What is it?" Seana asked, looking at the pill.

"Just follow orders."

"Orders, yeah," she said, thinking of the Army, and swallowed the pill.

Sometime later, as Seana drifted in and out of consciousness, she awoke to find Ari rubbing her neck with a fragrant oil. It felt extraordinarily good. *What was in that pill?* she wondered.

"Your blouse is getting all oily," he said solicitously. "Here, let me take it off for you..."

Seana fell asleep again. When her eyes opened next, she found she couldn't move. Ari had bound her wrists and ankles to the four-poster bed with fur-lined handcuffs, and was now massaging her naked body all over with oil. The red satin sheets around her appeared black where the oil had permeated. Outside it was nighttime. She had a flash of Marty's face. She briefly saw Shannon's face. *Stay with him,* Shannon said in her mind. *Stay with him,* she said in her mind, and fell back asleep.

When she awoke, Ari was now naked too and stood at the foot of the bed. Their eyes met.

"Date rape," she said bluntly.

"Nay, sister... you want to connect to The Leaders, merge with me," he said, believing that they would ride through him to enjoy her.

Although now a good soldier and trained to undergo any form of torture, including being raped, this all suddenly felt very wrong to her. Perhaps she should have asked Shannon to be more explicit with her. She assumed he meant to allow this to happen but what if she was wrong? What would this do to her, to Marty? She tested the strength of the handcuffs and found them not to be mere toys.

Ari smiled down at her helplessness.

God, please don't let this happen, she prayed with all her heart—prayer being the only remaining option she could see. Tears ran down her cheeks.

At that same moment, Templegard had just freed and extracted a captured Delta Force soldier and was in a submerged submarine in the Persian Gulf steaming back to a hospital ship. The ferocious firefight had been nearly a disaster and, although unhurt, he was exhausted and slept soundly in an upper bunk surrounded by snoring sailors.

In his dream, back on the familiar spaceship with his dream friends, he noticed one of the women was missing—not the dream woman he loved but rather the petite blonde with high cheekbones and lovely eyes. The others didn't seem to notice, but he felt there was something wrong, that she was in danger.

Still dreaming, he left the bridge and wandered inside the ship, seemingly being led.

On a real spacecraft hovering invisibly over North America, a Rebel Prince known as Admiral Jax watched as Ari Mann climbed onto the bed and onto Seana. Jax loosed a mild mindblast, flinging Ari off Seana and onto the floor, unconscious.

Seana gasped in amazement and a chill ran up her spine. *Did God intervene to save me?*

A moment later, a large man—a luminous larger-than-life godlike figure with daunting eyes and a red spade beard, dressed in a uniform that suggested he was a decorated officer—appeared at the foot of the bed, smiling down at her, and began to remove his uniform. She didn't know if she was dreaming or hallucinating from whatever was in that pill. She screamed.

Still being led in his dream, Templegard came into a cabin in the spaceship with a large four-poster bed, and there lay his missing companion, naked, handcuffed to the posts of the bed. In front of her loomed a large figure. His mind told him, *Rebel Prince*, although he didn't know what that meant.

Templegard tried to move forward to attack the figure but found that he couldn't move, as if paralyzed. He immediately called out for help. He couldn't remember the names of his companions but in his mind he screamed, *She's in trouble—we have a Rebel Prince on board—come to me now!*

Asleep in their respective beds, Shannon and Williams were both dreaming of being on a spacecraft with friends, when their dreams suddenly turned nightmarish. *Where was Seana? Wasn't she here a minute ago?* They each dreamed they had woken up and leaped from their beds, then had run through the spaceship corridors as if drawn to where Seana was in danger. They converged in the room where Templegard was paralyzed and saw each other, although they didn't recognize Templegard. They then saw Seana, tied to the bed and naked, crying. Ready to attack the giant who was stripping at the foot of the bed, they found they couldn't move. The three of them then instinctively mindblasted the giant.

The Rebel Prince laughed, unharmed, and removed the rest of his clothes. *Zombie Agents!* He guffawed at them. But then he found that *he* couldn't move. Shannon, Williams, and Templegard instinctively maintained their strongest mindblasts, which were sufficient to keep the Rebel from moving. *Damn!* Jax thought.

If any of the Theta men had remembered their true identities, their powers would have killed him, the Rebel realized. *He* knew who they were and he also knew that in their present lives they were totally unaware of being anything more than human—which, together with their bodies being in a dream state, reduced their powers greatly. Nevertheless, collectively they had enough power to freeze him in place. He looked longingly at the helpless naked woman in the bed, wanting her, but unable to have her.

He tried and failed to mindblast the three Agents and began to worry that his boss, Perse, would find him in this situation and demote him if not merely humiliate him. Shaken, he took the one remaining course of action open to him and managed to disappear entirely back up into Perse's ship *Planetkiller*.

Templegard, Shannon, and Williams woke up at different times, with slightly different memories of the dream fast fading. Templegard went over it in his mind and tried to fall back asleep into the same dream, but he slept lightly with no remembered dreams. Shannon woke up feeling immediate concern about Seana and called her mentally but got no response. He got out of bed and dressed. It was about 4 AM. Williams woke up minutes later feeling similarly concerned about Seana. He too called her in his mind. Hearing nothing back, he too jumped out of bed and quickly dressed.

When the naked giant disappeared, Seana had fainted.

Then she had the most lifelike dream she had ever had in her life. It seemed to be really happening. She was aboard a see-through holographic spacecraft, in bunk with the captain, when suddenly she recognized him as the naked giant, Jax. He was looking at her longingly but seemed unable to move any closer.

She woke up from the dream. Her limbs had been unbound. Ari was sleeping soundly beside her. She tried to stand up but fell back, and decided to go back to sleep. She went right back into the same dream. Now the captain was asleep on his bunk. She got off the bed and tiptoed around the cabin. She saw some weapons lying about, a closet of uniforms, a bathroom with various toiletries—all of which she could see in granular lifelike detail. She noticed a door that seemed to be made out of light and she stepped through it.

She found herself on a mezzanine overlooking a busy control bridge. Two larger-than-life officers, looking exactly like the captain, standing and talking on the mezzanine, noticed her and came over and spoke to her but their words were unintelligibly. She tried to ask them what they said but her own words also came out unintelligibly. The officers looked at each other, shrugged, and escorted her back through the door of light, where she saw the captain now awake in his bunk.

"Are you The Leaders?" she asked him, and he nodded with a smile.

"Did you send the transmission?" she asked, and he shook his head.

"But Ari and Otto said you did—"

"What do they know?" the captain roared good-naturedly, eyeing Seana's perky breasts. "Those bunglers down there... turn our gifts into weapons ...our good intentions into runaway evolution... our words into turds!"

The walls suddenly became completely transparent and Seana could see through the entire expanse of the immense spaceship. Nearby in the Officer's Club she saw many men who, again, looked just like the captain, laughing raucously.

"They're misinformed!" one of them declared.

"They're liars anyway!" another exclaimed.

Seana heard the sound of Ari's cough and woke up from the dream. She was back in his bed. The full moon looked directly in the window at her, casting a pearly tone to her skin. The clock read 4 AM. Ari was still out like a light and she now felt almost normal. She slipped gently off the bed, quickly toweled off as much of the oil as she could, dressed quietly, let herself out and descended in Ari's private elevator. The doorman smiled politely and hailed her a robocab.

The phone woke Ari up about an hour later. Seeing that Seana had let herself out, he picked up the phone.

"Only Otto would call me at 5 AM," he said into the phone.

Otto swept his eyes around his elegant suite in the Waldorf Towers and out at the setting full moon. Sitting at the desk, which was covered with pages of his fresh notes, he said to Ari, "I assume she's gone."

"A little while ago," Ari allowed guardedly, still wondering what actually had happened. Perhaps he should not have taken the Ecstasy too.

Otto laughed lecherously. "Get anything?"

"Otto, I think The Leaders had her, but they knocked me out so I don't really know."

This was Ari's best guess, and being psychic, fairly accurate, except the part about The Leaders having had Seana. Ari felt pretty bad about the whole mess now., He felt the burning sensation in his urethra that signaled "blue balls", so he knew he had come close to his goal. He'd hesitated when she started to cry, began losing his erection, and then passed out or been knocked out by The Leaders. When he woke up on the floor and got back into bed, he'd stayed awake long enough to free her limbs so she could at least sleep comfortably. He felt better about himself having done this.

"Hilarious!" Otto exclaimed, laughing roughly at Ari's expense, relishing the notion of the conceited young man getting his overdue comeuppance.

Ari took it manfully. "Guess I had it coming," he admitted. "At least I suspect the Army is going to finally leave me alone now. I connected her to The Leaders."

Otto blew up. "What?! Why did you do that?! Ari, I *told* you that you had become an embarrassment to me with The Leaders—now why are you making it worse, acting on your own initiative? Well, we're going to have a talk about this..." He trailed off on this threatening note.

Unseen by Otto was a small mark on the wall near him. On the other side of the wall in the adjacent suite, a tube-shaped amplifier protruded from the wall as if stuck there. Nastassia sat at a desk in that suite taking notes on the conversation, at least Otto's side of it.

"You can't call me tomorrow," she heard Otto say, and then, "I mean, I'm not home. No, I don't want *anyone* to know where I am at the moment—I'll explain when I see you. I'll come by in a day or so."

11

Shannon and Williams showed up in Theta's reception area almost simultaneously, not having spoken with each other since waking.

"Should one of us stay here and the other go to Mann's place?" Williams asked.

Shannon was about to respond when Seana flew in, went straight to Williams, and hugged him. He kissed her passionately. She turned and hugged Shannon, then hugged both of them at once.

"Thanks for saving me," she said huskily, close to tears. "Who was that other guy?"

"What?!" Shannon blurted.

Williams was similarly transfixed.

"Why don't we each tell what we experienced," Williams prompted, his body language suggesting Seana go first.

They moved into the conference room. Donna, somehow always already up before anyone else, materialized from nowhere to bring them coffee.

"Otto made it seem accidental but he gave me the edge of his hand to my neck, I fell, and was nearly trampled, but Mr. Brain saved me," she said, using Ari's nickname sardonically. "He then drove me to his place in his fancy car, showing off by shifting gears with his left hand so he could rub my neck with his right hand. He carried me in to his building and took me straight to his bedroom, laying me on the bed on the pretext of massaging my neck. Then he gave me some kind of pill—and I think he took one too, maybe not the same kind—anyway, I got woozier, then found myself naked, chained to the bed, and covered with massage oil. Just as he was ready to jump my bones, he passed out. It was weird, though—from the way he fell, it actually looked like he had been clobbered by something invisible."

The three looked at each other in wonderment.

"What happened next was much weirder. A giant man materialized at the foot of the bed and started taking his uniform off. For some reason, I took him to be the captain of The Leaders' spaceship. Then you two came in with another guy and had some kind of a mental face-off with him. I tried to help but didn't know how I could. Anyway, his body seemed paralyzed, but he kept making a head-butting motion, which for some reason caused me to say to myself *mindblast*, but nothing seemed to happen. Eventually he dematerialized. I fainted. I guess you guys had something else to do because you weren't there when I woke up."

They shook their heads as if in disbelief, though they knew better.

"Funny because I prayed to God for help, thinking S/He would send you two." She paused for a moment, a sacred pause.

"But before I woke up," she went on, remembering, "I had the most bizarre dream, almost humorous. It wasn't scary for some reason. I had a sense of not being at risk anymore. I was on the captain's spaceship, in his cabin. He was asleep in his bunk. Maybe I astral traveled—although I've never done that before—I looked around and saw very detailed views as if in real life, not the vagueness of a dream. I left his cabin and started to wander into the spaceship but two crewmen escorted me back to his quarters, our only words unintelligible as we couldn't understand each other's language. The captain was awake when I came back in and we talked and somehow we *could* understand each other. And then later in the dream, when the walls became transparent and I could see men all over the ship who looked exactly like the captain, laughing and making witty remarks, I could understand them too."

The two men shook their heads again, amazed by Seana's dream that maybe wasn't a dream after all.

"What did you learn? Are they Otto's 'Leaders'?" Shannon asked.

"They have been in communication with Otto and Ari, so yes," Seana said, "but he said they were *not* the source of the transmission. He and his crew called Otto and Ari and their fascist group, bunglers and liars."

She appeared to have concluded recounting her perspective on the surreal events.

"We were never there in person," Shannon told her, and Williams nodded.

A chill went down Seana's spine and the hair stood up on the back of her neck.

Body language suggested Shannon go next so he did. "I was asleep. I started worrying about you in a dream, about you being in trouble. In the dream I was wandering around in a spaceship that I think I've seen in other dreams, and you were lost and I was looking for you. Then I came into a cabin in which you were tied to a bed with a giant looming over you. I saw Williams there and another guy who looked familiar, maybe a Delta Force guy or a SEAL I knew. The three of us looked at each other and went to lunge at the giant but we couldn't move. Then we tried mentally to paralyze him and it worked. We were in a Mexican standoff and then the giant just disappeared—you know, like people disappear in dreams. I couldn't sleep after that so I got up, dressed, and came down here. That's when I ran into you two."

"My experience was very similar to yours," Williams said to Shannon, "except that the third guy was never very clear to me. He felt like a friend but I couldn't really make out what he looked like." Williams was apparently satisfied with his testimony.

"So what really happened?" Shannon asked matter-of-factly.

"The only way it makes sense is that all three of us, under pressure of this horrific situation, astral traveled for the first time," Seana said.

"Actually I think I astral traveled twice when I was twelve years old," Williams disclosed. "But I agree with you. If you, Shannon, and I were just dreaming, then why did we all see the same giant and the same unknown ally? Too much coincidence for it to be random chance or just a dream."

"Well, that part of it is exciting," Shannon said to himself, thinking of Congressman Baynes and the battle for the budget appropriation for Theta.

The three of them paused for a moment, reflecting on their revelations, overawed by the turn of events: achieving astral travel, what might be a real spacecraft with real aliens hovering invisibly above Earth, mindblasts—whatever they were, the ally who had appeared to each of them... sensing that whatever they had stumbled upon could be vastly bigger than anything they had ever imagined.

"What else has been going on since the fracas at the UN?" Seana asked them. "Where are Khan and Jason?"

"Khan texted me a few minutes ago," Shannon said. "Jason isn't answering his page, and Khan is trying to find him."

Seana speculated, "Gone AWOL?"

Shannon shook his head. "Jase most likely went after the mystery woman he saw during the transmission—the woman in the window. He saw her at the UN."

"He was just about to go over to her before the Danang Lama came out but I held him back," Williams added.

Shannon took Otto's sunglasses out of his pocket and laid them on the conference table.

"Otto's sunglasses—" Seana recognized them at once.

"Yes," Shannon agreed. "No metal parts, so they evaded the metal detectors. They shoot a plastic explosive-driven ceramic bullet with another plastic explosive payload in the bullet."

"So Otto is the one who shot at the Danang Lama?!" Seana exclaimed.

"Right," Shannon said. "Lab's checking Otto's fingerprints right now."

"But why?!" Seana asked.

Shannon shrugged.

"Does Ari know that Otto was the shooter?"

"No way of knowing," Shannon said. "Otto didn't go back to his hotel room, and we don't know where the hell he is. I want you to go back and hang out with Mr. Brain again soon—it's our best shot at reconnecting with Otto."

Shannon glanced over at Williams, relieved to see he was not upset.

"I don't think Ari will go for a rerun anytime soon," Williams said with conviction, knowing he would severely hurt Ari if he did.

Seana nodded in agreement, fearless given her confidence in her two strong defenders—her lover, and her boss, with whom she also felt a secret attraction.

"Before we send you back in, we'll see if Khan and Jason can get to Otto through Ari. Whenever Khan finds Jason, that is," Shannon added.

"What can the Danang Lama tell us about all this?" Seana asked.

"Nothing, since he's disappeared too," Williams replied. "I tried to follow him but he seemed to evaporate into thin air. Unless he turned himself into *this*—" Williams said, putting the still-luminous rose on the conference table.

"We got a report later that he's been kidnapped for his own protection by a fanatical sect of his followers," Shannon added, his sour face suggesting he had his doubts.

"Ari said Marty shot him," Seana said and laughed, "when the Danang Lama started to say 'There are not one but many Gods'—"

Williams shook his head, appalled though not surprised.

"He was actually about to say that there are two sources of psychic information vying for control of Earth," Williams proclaimed, based on his own compass. "As in a propaganda war. *The Message* of the transmission came from the good side."

Put off by this undocumented assertion, Shannon countered, "How do *you* know? Your sense of certainty is dangerous, Marty!"

Ω

Nastassia laid out on the desk recognizable sketches of Otto, Ari, and Jason, two she had brought from Russia and the Otto one new, sketched after seeing him at the UN.

Realizing who had fired the shot at the Danang Lama, she had followed that one person going the opposite direction from the crowd. She could read the guilt in his face. She had no idea who he was but in the absence of anything better to do, she had followed him.

His destination was the Waldorf Towers, where she observed him checking in. After he stepped into the Tower elevator, the door closing behind him, she had checked in with the same clerk who, distracted by her unusual features, didn't notice her in his mind manipulating him so as to give her the closest empty suite to Otto. By luck that empty suite was right next door.

She had quickly gone to work, mounting an amplifier on the shared wall, and had been listening to him mumbling to himself as he thought aloud in his hotel room, capturing some of it on hotel notepaper. Including his call to Ari in the predawn hours following the shooting.

She had no fixed game plan. She'd had fleeting thoughts about eluding the Russians trailing her, and disappearing into Western society, but her parents would be tortured in reprisal, so that was not a choice she would ever make. She would rather take pain on herself than cause it in others.

Her hope had been that she would be directed in some way at the UN meeting as to how to contact the source of the transmission. This hunch was her provisional interpretation of what was happening.

Fortunately her bosses had equipped her with standard high-tech spyware and enough training to be able to do whatever she might need to do, like tap into Otto's suite so as to be able to eavesdrop on the would-be killer. She learned that he believed in some mysterious Leaders who could have been the natural source of the transmission. So she needed to continue to observe him and learn more about these Leaders.

In her lifelong reading of esoteric literature, Nastassia had come across similar concepts. She'd concluded intuitively that Earth people had been contacted by more advanced beings throughout human history and that those "advanced" beings probably did not all come from the same place. She sensed having learned this truth in many lives before this one.

This man Otto didn't seem to realize that there is more than one set of Leaders.

The amplified sound coming in from next door together with the pen scratching on the paper muffled the almost inau- dible sound of someone opening the door and slipping in silently, closing the door soundlessly.

Nastassia's psychic senses picked up on the entry and she spun from her chair into a fighting crouch.

The man made warding gestures to forestall violence. She looked more closely and recognized him as the man she had seen in the window during the transmission, whom she knew had been her lover in a past life in France. She reminded her- self that he was not the man of her dreams, her soul mate, the man she always dreamed about and would find some day and keep herself chaste for until then.

"My name is Jason Page now," he said, stepping forward slowly so as not to alarm her. His face emerged into the light, looking at her adoringly and managing to conceal his guilt at having released a video bug that would fly up through the darkness to a perch near the ceiling, providing an optimal view of the room.

"Stop there," she said when he was little more than arm's length away, and he reluctantly did.

"I have to tell you something," she said in a gentle voice. "I know we were lovers once, but I am betrothed to another now."

Jason's dream collapsed suddenly and his face fell. He sank back into a chair, covering his face with shame and disillusion.

"I still love you, darling," Jason said softly. "What am I to do?"

Nastassia stepped closer and touched his arm. "We can still be friends."

He laughed ruefully once, then touched her hand and looked up at her.

"I guess that's more than I deserve," he said.

"What do you mean?" she asked, sitting across from him in an identical chair.

"You deserve a better man than me," Jason said. "If I truly love you, which I do, then I want you to be with a man who can really make you happy. I can't even make myself happy. I'm not a very nice person. And yet, inside, I can now remember that I am a very good person, but somehow it doesn't come through."

She read in his mind that he had sensed during the transmission being told he had been Jesus Christ. That thought had been implanted by some lower-level being, she felt; it did not resonate with her truth sense that he had been Jesus. Perhaps there had been different transmissions happening at the same time?

How could she take him down from his false belief that he was Jesus? It would be unkind to avoid the matter because that belief would likely get him in big trouble. It would raise expectations that could never be fulfilled. Ultimately it would hurt him, scar him, in ways that could last many lifetimes. She couldn't keep her mouth shut and live with herself.

"Jason, my name is Nastassia now," she started.

"It had been Nikki," he said.

She nodded. "You have to be careful about what you hear in your head," she said. "You have to leave things on the dashboard of your mind as possible truths without fully believing them. Let evidence accumulate. Test it. Then you can form stronger convictions but always leaving a grain of salt. It may be true, it may not be true."

"You mean even *you* don't believe that I am Jesus," Jason said to himself miserably.

She inferred that he meant "even she who had at least some love for him". It was true. Nastassia had at least some love for everybody, even her treacherous lecherous atheist bosses.

"You and I and everybody are actually all the same person—the One Consciousness that plays all roles," Nastassia said, disclosing to him what she saw as the ultimate secret of all time.

He looked up as if not understanding.

"It doesn't matter whether you were Jesus or not, because all of us are the same One Consciousness—One Being." Nastassia spelled out her thought.

He seemed bemused but open-minded, disposed to place faith in whatever she said because he saw her as the ultimate goddess whom he not only wanted and loved but actually worshipped.

She offered him something to drink from the minibar and they both opted for vodka tonic. They sat quietly for a moment, sipping, absorbing so much information and letting things settle between them.

"Jason," she began and their eyes met.

"Nastassia," he said.

"You are part of Theta, and I am part of Psycho Division One," she said, having read his mind and also having got the same information from him during the transmission.

"I know," he said, remembering their exchange during the transmission.

"How do we play that?" she asked.

"Damned if I know. Do you want to defect?"

"In a New York minute, except they have my parents."

He smiled that she knew the term. She learned it in Russian Spy School. Then he dropped the smile, thinking of her parents' grim situation.

"Maybe we could help extricate them?" Jason said, suddenly excited like a child. She smiled sadly.

"My dream as well," she confessed, "for someday, when I can figure out how to do that without a lot of people getting killed."

"We could help you," Jason said. "We have resources."

"I'm tempted. But I am probably bugged here as we speak. And chances are that all I get for even entertaining such a discussion is major trouble. It's a chicken egg thing. I can't know if you guys are really up to it or not without playing along with you for so long that the odds of my getting caught become astronomically high. I do know how competent the Russian spy agencies are, while yours to me are relatively unknown. You'd have to convince me by telling me secrets. I could be a double agent. The whole idea feels like a dangerous rathole. Let's speak no more of it," she said firmly.

Knowing that they might even be videoing her by now, she didn't wink or give any visible signal beyond her words. He had no idea that she did not mean every word she said. In fact, she was trying to play it both ways as far as she safely could, actually more open to considering the rescue alternative than she could make obvious. She knew Jason didn't get it but she left it where it was for the moment.

"Furthermore," she said, "I've got work to do. I'm not here to work against the interests of the United States, I'm here— fully legal—doing investigations into the worldwide phenomenon known as the transmission or *The Message*, for the lawful benefit of my own country. And I don't want you guys spying on me too. I like it little enough with my own people spying on me, like when I'm in the shower, naked—I want to save that for my betrothed as much as I can. So I have to now ask you politely and not unlovingly to leave. I'm afraid we won't be seeing each other again, except at things like the UN event and other such gatherings."

"That doesn't sound much like being friends to me," Jason said.

"It's uncomfortable for me in my current situation, and could even be dangerous for me, to hang out with you as much as you'd like. It will cause me to have to do a lot of explaining. At best we'll have to ration seeing each other. I know you don't want to make my life a living hell—any more than it already is," she overacted and vacillated at the same time. Having a friend and a lifeline to the Americans was not something she wanted to cut off.

Jason stood and took her hands in his. They cheek kissed and he went for the second cheek too. He knew enough to stop there, and left, heartbroken.

Ω

The sound of Otto working stopped and he got ready to move. Nastassia knew he would eventually venture out on some mission or just to stave off cabin fever, and so she was ready to leave instantly to follow him. She stepped into her shoes and listened. He seemed to be heading purposefully toward the door. She carefully drew the amplifier out of the wall so as not to increase the size of the mark, tossed it in her bag and got up, moving swiftly to the door. She waited until she heard his door open, then opened hers and stepped out into the hall. He nodded perfunctorily at her and walked toward the elevators, with Nastassia not far behind.

He held the elevator door as she turned the corner and sped up to get in. "Thanks!" she said cheerily, in the manner of a teenager, and Otto merely smiled back then looked forward, ignoring her. So young, she would obviously be a boring conversationalist, and besides, he could afford to buy girls like her for a night but preferred someone he could relate to. He felt edgy, wanting to be left alone, not his usual extraverted self. At the lobby she purposely walked toward Lexington, so he could get ahead of her going toward Park, then she made a show of catching herself having gone the wrong way, turned and headed toward Park, his back still in sight.

Jason stayed well behind, following Nastassia from a distance. In the hustle and bustle of the hotel lobby, her focus on following Otto without his detection, she never picked up on Jason.

Small robocabs, designed for one passenger, lined up to the right at the corner of Park Avenue, four of them taking up the space of two cars. Otto got in the first robocab and she got in the second. Jason got in the third. Khan appeared, walking around the corner from Fiftieth Street onto Park and took the fourth.

Nastassia being a silly little girl to him, Otto never gave her another thought, his mind racing with alternative schemes and counter schemes to get out of the noose he'd put himself in and back to his normal life. She had the robocab follow him up Park, knowing intuitively that he'd be going to Ari Mann's place.

So focused on what was ahead, she did not cover her six. She could have easily detected Jason if she'd placed her attention situational 360 instead of anticipatory forward. Her training was not at fault; her attachment to the outcome of the showdown she anticipated having next had distracted her from remembering her training.

Nastassia suddenly saw herself as a little girl. In fact, she was just sixteen now, though looking probably twenty-one to most men; her cover showed her as nineteen. The guy who tried to kill the Danang Lama was obviously a ruthless killer, and a psychic or he wouldn't have gotten into the UN Diplomats Lounge for the event. She had no idea how she would stack up against him. She knew that she would be disadvantaged by not wanting to hurt him.

What about the other guy, Ari? She had seen him during the transmission but other than him being rich, she had no feel for who or what he might be. He could be equally dangerous or worse than Otto. Why was a little girl being sent in to get information from men like that?

She laughed at herself. She knew it was just her nervously excited internal babble calling her a little girl. She turned it off.

The GRU Spetsnaz agents back in the lobby of Nastassia's hotel had detected Jason's interest in her, which earned him a permanent two-man tail. They were behind the robocab convoy but in a cab with a human driver.

The other GRU Spetsnaz team, who had gotten the last suite on Nastassia's floor, were already inspecting her suite. They already knew the video and audio bugging was functioning perfectly but they wanted to get Jason's fingerprints and some closeups of her drawings.

"Why are we doing this," one asked the other. "She's Division One, isn't she?"

"Stop trying to think," the other one answered.

Other GRU Spetsnaz had taken firing positions to hit targets in most of the rooms of Ari's suite and out on the terrace, as well as in Nastassia's suite at the Waldorf. Vertical envelopment specialists waited by copters atop 200 Park, at the Copter Club. Other helicopter aficionados were irritated that someone had taken up all the parking space for copters at 200 Park—bought it out for the next two months. Grumbling could be heard from as far away as Connecticut's posh Gold Coast towns.

Another GRU Spetsnaz held the controls that could blow up the plastic explosive device hidden in Nastassia's copious bag, where it was hard to find anything anyway.

A plan suddenly popped into Nastassia's head, and she thanked whoever sent it. It was Templegard, in fact, dreaming about her while sleeping comfortably in an expensive suite in Tokyo.

As Otto's robocab and hers pulled up in front of Ari's building, Nastassia fumbled to pay so that Otto could disappear inside before she stepped out of the cab. Following the plan from somewhere, she went over to what had been Otto's cab and looked inside, pretended to see something, then opened the door and stuck her upper body in and came out again, holding in her hand an expensive-looking Maltese Cross money clip with U.S. twenties in it. It was her own.

She went up to the doorman, who had observed her movements and who now looked at her quizzically. She handed him the money clip. "The man who just came in—he left this in the cab," she explained.

"Why that's Mr. Wagner—he went up to Mr. Mann's penthouse—I'll bring it to him," the doorman blabbed, saying more than he normally would to a stranger, for some reason unbeknownst to him.

Nastassia had gently pulled it out of him. Secretly disappointed that she did not get invited in to present it herself, she turned over the money clip. She walked West into Central Park and sat down on the grass to think about her next move. It was a gorgeous day, with squirrels, birds, and butterflies all around. Dragonflies came and sat on her hands. This felt like heaven compared to living deep underground beneath a mountain. Blissed out, she stopped thinking about the mission for a while.

Ari, wearing a purple brocade bathrobe to breakfast, came back from briefly answering the door, his butler being off somewhere hiring the mercs Ari had ordered. He handed the money clip to Otto as he rejoined him in the breakfast nook.

"Never saw it before," Otto said, taking the money clip and counting the money. "Could use the two hundred bucks though!" he kidded. Otto was a billionaire. He claimed to have inherited it but Ari had his suspicions about Otto moving stolen art. He had come into possession of incredible rare works of art by the masters from Otto and it all stood up to scrupulous chain of custody verification. Ari had no idea how Otto had been able to garner so much great art, which is what had made him believe Otto's story about The Leaders in the first place.

"Who is she?" Ari asked him, chomping again into his eggs béarnaise. "The doorman said she's Eurasian looking, maybe a teenager, hard to tell—"

Otto's eyes widened and he sat up straight. "I don't know who she is—she's in the suite next to me—she could have followed me to the hotel." He started to breathe hard. "See, Ari—that's why The Leaders told me I couldn't go home—someone is after me. I don't know why."

Nastassia felt a sudden urge to go back to Ari's building—quickly. Too bad it had only been a few minutes of great peace. She leaped up and ran two blocks then slowed to normal New Yorker pace for the last ten yards. As she reached the corner, Otto came out of Ari's building and started to walk south. She followed him from the other side of Park Avenue, without appearing to be paying any attention to him, looking around as if from out of town.

She stopped and leaned against a building, pretending to be talking on her cellphone as she saw him about to cross to her side of the avenue. She waited until she saw him disappear to the right, heading west onto a short side street. She got to the corner quickly and saw him descend into an alleyway below street level. Afraid the alleyway would go all the way to the next street and she might lose him, she followed him down into the darkness. Her eyes, not yet adjusted from the bright sunlight, were not much use. She had just started to put out psychic feelers when, moving swiftly through the dark dank passage, she turned a corner to find him standing there, pointing a small gun at her.

"And who might you be, my dear?" Otto asked, then snapped at her. "Down on your knees, hands clasped on your head."

She complied reluctantly.

"Good. Now answer," he ordered.

"I want to meet Mr. Brain—I read about him recently on the Internet," she said, which was true. "Can you arrange it?"

Otto paused and then laughed. "Cute—nice try. But now who are you really?"

She stared sullenly at him, which he found coquettish and arousing.

"Aren't you a little too obviously Russian to work undercover in the States?"

"Who are *you* working for? Or are you acting out your own personal psychotic opera?" Nastassia heard herself say, although she felt it didn't sound like her.

This immediately enraged Otto. He threateningly cocked the hammer on his gun, hoping to scare her into submission while quickly evaluating scenarios including what he could do to her for his personal needs. The cocking of the gun and her reading his thoughts did succeed in scaring her. She reacted instinctively, her training kicking into high gear.

From Otto's point of view she seemed to disappear and instantly reappear behind him, chopping the gun out of his hand, and hitting and kicking him in rapid fire. He went down quickly, not quite senseless. As she drew closer, he released a puff of gas from out of his sleeve into her face and she collapsed, wheezing for breath. He beat a hasty retreat, abandoning his gun.

Nastassia managed to catch enough breath to get up, escaping from the underground passage back into fresh air, her eyes tearing, her breath still gasping. She went back into Central Park, to the lake, and washed her hands and face in it. She realized the lake wasn't all that clean but it did help her eyes recover.

12

Ari, still in his purple brocade bathrobe and enjoying the fine day, happy to be alone and unbothered on his terrace, sipped a mimosa and waited for tips from his psychic benefactors.

Cholmondeley appeared, announcing, "There's a Miss Petrova to see you, sir, from the Russian Embassy."

"Miss Petrova, eh?" Ari said, sipping his drink. "Sounds like Otto's friend—I'll see her out here."

The butler returned a moment later with Nastassia, now adorned with large dragonfly earrings. Ari stood and shook her hand.

"Mr. Mann, Miss Petrova," Cholmondeley said.

"Please sit down, Miss Petrova," Ari said and held the chair for her at the umbrellaed table.

She gratefully sat and he pushed her chair in gently.

"What's this all about?" he asked amiably. "Champagne?" he asked and she nodded, so he poured her some in the empty glass the butler had made appear on the table imperceptibly minutes ago. "Orange juice too?" he asked and she shook her head, wanting to appear naughty. He filled the rest of her glass and clinked with her.

"I'm with the Russian Embassy," she said. "I was at the UN yesterday when the attempt was made on the Danang Lama's life."

He nodded, eschewing the obvious remark 'aren't you a little young...', instead saying agreeably, "Yes, so was I."

"Were you there with someone?" Nastassia asked too bluntly and too soon, inexperienced as she was.

Ari smiled at her over-eager naivete, charmed with the girl, entertaining fantasies though wary that she might be a minor and of course he wouldn't want bad publicity.

"Why do you ask?" he responded. "I mean, is this an official Russian investigation, or something else? Incidentally, can I see your credentials?"

"Of course," she said, and started to rummage through her bottomless bag.

"By the way, those are the most unusual earrings," Ari said, enjoying watching her every move. "I like them."

Nastassia had forgotten about her earrings. "Oh yes," she acknowledged, pausing from the burrowing to speak to her earrings. "Okay children, that's enough for today—there's your park over there—" she pointed to Central Park. The two live dragonflies shook themselves out of trance and flew off toward the park, chasing each other playfully along their way.

Ari stared at the scene with amazement and as the dragonflies disappeared in the distance he gazed at her, gobsmacked. She handed him her Embassy ID, and he glanced at it and handed it back. She put it away, noticing him looking at her differently now.

"You look familiar... yes," he said. "I saw you... the day they boosted the power. You looked more French then. Now you look like a Eurasian Latina."

She lit up. "You got it!" she said. "You were naked in a hot tub."

"Jacuzzi," he corrected.

"Yes, I have one too, at... home," she said truthfully. The base actually did have a Jacuzzi-branded hot tub.

"Where were you?" he asked, then smiled. "Naked in yours?"

She tittered briefly. "I was in Russia," she said simply, playing along.

"You're here investigating the transmission," he surmised, and she nodded. "Well, I could tell you something about it, but I'd need the permission of the U.S. government first."

She smiled at him girlishly. From Ari's point of view, he zoomed in on her eyes as she made them more beautiful for him. From Nastassia's point of view, Ari was transfixed by her eyes and could not look away, much as he tried.

"The Leaders—" Ari began in a strangled voice, being forced to speak against his will.

She released him and he looked away. He finished his glass pensively and refilled both their glasses.

"You pulled that out of me. I don't like that... don't think you'll be able to do that again," he said with bravado. He stared at her, his face hard. Another part of him getting hard too.

She stared back. She had a momentary vision of them making love and realized he had projected that to her as a subliminal hypnotic suggestion. She laughed.

"Excellent mind shield, Mr. Brain," she commended him. "I won't do it anymore. There's really nothing you can tell me... I've heard the story before."

"'Story?'"

"Yes, The Leaders... the story is not the whole truth," she said.

Ari suddenly had enough and lost his cool.

"It's not, eh?!" he exclaimed, and threw his glass against the brick façade of the building near the French doors, where it shattered into a hundred tiny pieces.

"N—" she started to say but he lunged at her.

From his point of view she seemed to disappear and suddenly he was going over the parapet to a long fall down to the street and certain death. She pulled him back by his silk pajama pants, drove her hand into his stomach, chopped him behind the head, and he went dark.

Ω

When Ari recovered consciousness he found himself manacled to his four-poster bed, stark naked. He found this immediately arousing, with the usual effect. He noted that his ankles were joined together rather than spread-eagled.

"I prefer the Crucifixion position, don't you?" Nastassia asked him, sipping her champagne. She had brought the bucket with them.

Where was Chumley? Ari wondered. *Oh yeah, I gave him the night off. But he usually never actually leaves...*

"How... do you jump through space like that?" he asked her.

"I don't... but somehow I can cloud men's minds for a moment," she replied truthfully.

"What are you up to?" he asked, clearly puzzled. "I thought you said there was no information I could give you."

"Who said anything about information? It's been a long assignment," Nastassia said teasingly. She began to slowly remove her clothes, stopping to finish her glass and refill it. He noticed she had found the refrigerator and opened a new bottle. He became more and more aroused until he could not take his eyes off her for a second. She somehow had found his stash of sex toys and was flipping his toy whip back and forth as she moved enticingly around the room, stripping. He heard his breath and his heart respond to her tactics but he was enjoying it and didn't sense any danger.

She came up to him, her face very close to his and her breath sweet and nutty from the Veuve Clicquot. "You've been a very, very, bad, bad boy here, Ari," she told him, drawing the whip across his chest, at which his erection bobbed.

"What do you mean, baby?" he asked her breathlessly.

"I sense that you had a sister of mine entrapped the way I have you, right here, in the same way, not so long ago," she said. "You would have taken her against her will if something hadn't stopped you, wouldn't you?"

Ari was forced to admit it. "Yes, and I am so sorry that I was such a brute," he improvised, hoping this would not keep her from having her way with him. "I promise never to do such a thing again to any woman," he said, half sincerely. He could sense a subtle though still nearly imperceptible change in himself, to seemingly becoming more aware.

"Hmm..." she said noncommittally. Removing the last of her outer clothes, she came closer, approaching so that the body parts that attracted him the most were within inches of him. He strained against his bonds but could not make tactile contact. He looked lustfully at her purple lace thong and bra. She had picked those things up her first day in New York at the upscale Journelle Lingerie and loved wearing them today for the first time. The tag had said "Merlot", which she didn't know was a type of wine but assumed it was some kind of purple plant life.

"I'm going to do you a big favor, Mr. Brain," she said, "because you're not such a bad guy. But you're never going to learn your lessons if you're let off too easy. Someday you'll thank me for this," she said.

He began to imagine that she was going to rape him in a way that would hurt. Maybe stick something up his butt. He wondered what she had in mind, imagining it would be more fun than not. He had tried every hetero approach he could think of so far but this was something new so he found himself looking forward to whatever it might be.

She looked through his sex toys and found a few interesting things. She carried these behind her as she approached him. He expected something exotic but as it turned out, giggling like a child, she sprayed him copiously with baby oil straight out of the bottle. He closed his eyes and mouth as the spray came up to his face and then opened his eyes again as she sprayed him everywhere else, soaking the silk sheets yet again.

Next she stuck two pills in his mouth, which he knew from the shape and color to be high-dose Viagra.

"Ah—wait—that's too big a dose—" he tried to say but she shook her head a certain way and offered him a sip of champagne, so he swallowed them. Clearly he didn't need them.

Finally he saw her trying to figure out the cock ring. He was going to explain it to her but suddenly she got it and came closer and slid it on, careful to not touch him. Once it was on,

she turned the fabric dial to tighten it. Now he was ready—
he felt certain he would love whatever happened next. He
breathed heavily, his eyes unable to move off of her.

She moved around the bedroom as if doing a very slow
form of modern dance mixed with Tai Chi. Ari was riveted,
finding it erotic. Nastassia reached out her mind to contact her
dream lover, wanting to do this teasing dance for him, for his
enjoyment.

Templegard, hanging upside down in a Turkish prison,
was not so much asleep as knocked unconscious—but still
able to dream. In his dream she came to him and he felt his
strength coming back. He sent her powerful waves of love and
she moaned softly.

So did Ari. He was by now writhing on the bed, trying to
get free. "How much money would you like, dear?" he asked
her. She ignored him and pretended to have an orgasm in the
dance, almost singing her moans of pleasure. He made invol-
untary noises, mostly around the syllable Oh.

She segued out of her dance and traipsed around, found
the champagne, poured herself more, and took a sip. "I want to
meet The Leaders, as you call them," she said.

"Why didn't you say so!" he exclaimed, smiling, certain that
he had her now. "I can arrange that, for a little quid pro quo."

She had never heard that term but read his mind to get the
meaning. She came closer, looked into his eyes sweetly, and
said softly, "Nothing for you, I'm afraid, my friend. I'm saving
it for my true love."

"How do you know I'm not him?" he asked and she just
smiled. She didn't want to hurt his feelings. She never wanted
to hurt anyone's feelings.

She resumed her dance. To her, this was a new art form
coming through her. She had no idea what her next move
would be, the dance was doing itself. Again, for some reason
not clear to her, she pretended to have an orgasm enhanced
with song. This was all very interesting, especially given how
strong her libido had been recently. It seemed harmless fun

but perhaps it was intended to teach Ari not to take women against their will.

"Oh no..." he said weakly. "I thought it was my turn, finally."

"That's it, keep begging, Mr. Brain. My sisters and I like the sound of you begging, for a change," Nastassia said, hoping that the women he had mistreated could somehow be looking in.

"I don't know if this is healthy," he bemoaned, thinking of his recent case of blue balls.

Nastassia laughed gently. "Look down, sisters... he doesn't look so high and mighty now, does he? The poor guy... I think we may have finally broken his arrogance..."

At that moment Ari flashed that he was Seana and Nastassia was him. He felt a sense of violation and weakness. He was experiencing this, at Nastassia's hand, to give him the same feeling of powerlessness and worthlessness that he must have forced upon Seana. This was his just repayment. He *was* a brute, someone who would always take advantage of women.

He suddenly saw his low behavior for what it was. How could he have let himself be that way for so long? It was unthinkable. He had been so unconscious of himself. He felt thoroughly humiliated. His towering ego collapsed. He felt like the uncertain little boy with all the crazy ideas and people always laughing at him and making him feel small. He had never really changed, he had just covered up his real self with this act he played out, and he had fooled himself long ago into believing the act was the real thing.

"It must be exhausting to be you," Nastassia ventured, reading his mind.

"Yes," Ari admitted, thinking of the night Seana came to his place for the first time. To impress her, he never stopped moving for a moment, showing off all his talents. *How pathetic,* he thought, *and yes, it's a lot of effort, driven by nothing but festering old memories that don't even reach the surface of my mind.*

"As a Jew, you must believe in God," Nastassia said out of the blue.

"Not really," Ari said.

She was flabbergasted. "You mean, you're not a practicing Jew, just born Jewish?"

"Something like that," Ari said, proud to be an atheist. "I still say I'm a Jew..."

"So that more people will like you," Nastassia said, and he nodded miserably in self-loathing. She felt sorry to be bringing up these feelings in him but trusted that this whole process would ultimately leave him a better person.

"So you believe the universe was accidental, and came out of nowhere?" she asked.

"Of course. In infinite time, everything has to happen," Ari said.

"Not true," Nastassia said. "I bet if you sat on a beach for infinite time, you'd never see the ocean throw up a perfect sandcastle at the water's edge."

Ari hadn't thought of it that way before and pondered the image, forgetting his lust for a moment.

"Why do The Leaders say they sent *The Message*?" Nastassia asked.

"They don't tell me anything," Ari said self-contemptuously.

"What did you get out of *The Message*?" Nastassia asked.

"It was just stepped-up power, my dear," Ari said to her in a loving tone. "I'm afraid it's all these religious types that have projected their own messages onto it."

She shook her head. "If that were the case, then we are somehow illogically all projecting the same content into it—all our stories agree, across Christians, Buddhists, Muslims, Jews, Taoists, Wiccans, and lots of other religious sects with diverging doctrines. For the first time in history all these people are telling the same story."

"And what is that story?" he wanted to know.

"There is only One Self, and it is inside all of us, it IS all of us, we are all that one thing together," Nastassia said. "I knew this to be true before *The Message*."

Considering that concept open-mindedly for the first time, Ari eventually said, "I can see how that could be true, but first I would have to accept that mind came before matter."

She nodded vigorously.

"This experience I am having of looking out from inside an apparently separate body," he went on, "if I take that to be the ultimate reality, this selfness I experience, then I can imagine it's possible that we are all one field of consciousness, partitioned into these apparently separate selves..."

Nastassia saw him beginning to wake up ethically. Her role playing had done its job. She didn't need any more information than she had already gotten out of him, and she had no desire to meet The Leaders, as he called them. She had a deep intuition of who they were and what her relationship was with them—they were ancient enemies. Meeting them would be the last thing she wanted. She felt certain they were not the source of the transmission, which she believed certainly came from beings who knew of the oneness of all things as she did. That's what *The Message* was all about.

Her mission was to find out and meet whoever sent it, and Ari was a cold trail in that regard. Now she didn't know what to do. She had been going with the flow of events that had led her here with Ari, sure that the beings who looked out for her would bring her to where she needed to go. So far they had led her to meet deluded people with their own agendas, certainly good to know about so as to look out for them in the future. But her parents' lives depended upon her satisfying her bosses by connecting with the source of the transmission. Nothing came to mind as to how to go about doing that, or where to go from here. She sighed.

The cellphone rang and she picked it up, pressed the button to connect to the caller, and held the phone to Ari's ear.

"Hello," Ari said. "Yes, hello Otto. No I'm feeling fine thanks," he said in a monotone. "What? All right... see you soon."

He looked up at Nastassia. "You can hang up now."

"You didn't tell him I was here," she observed, amused.

"He'll see for himself soon enough," Ari said, as if resigned to his current fate.

She smiled and headed for the shower—some of that baby oil had landed on her.

When she had left the room, Ari raised his voice just slightly and said into the air, "Chumley, please come get me out of this thing."

The butler came in a minute later and noted his boss's situation. *Blue balls again, boss?* Ari thought he heard in his mind, not sure if he was just imagining it. Cholmondeley approached, keeping his eyes averted, saw the keys and unlocked the manacles. Ari got up and put on his vivid purple bathrobe and headed to his office to await Otto. The butler changed the sheets and tidied up as Ari left the room.

13

Ari's erection was still dwindling as he faced off with Otto across Ari's broad office desk. He had forgotten to take off the cock ring until Otto's elevator was on its way up, then he stuffed the thing in a bathrobe pocket.

"You idiot!" Otto screamed at him. "She tried to *kill* me this morning, and here you are entertaining her in your bed all afternoon—"

Confused at this revelation and at the fast pace of events, Ari instinctively changed the subject to gain time. "Otto, what's your connection with the assassination attempt?"

"*No* connection, but somebody's trying to pin it on me," Otto retorted hotly.

"Why?"

"I don't know! But it's someone who's working against The Leaders."

"How do the Russians fit in?" Ari prodded.

"I don't know!" Otto roared in frustration. "Get her in here and let's find out!" Their eyes met.

Ari went to the bedroom and found Nastassia almost dressed.

"Is Otto here?" she asked sweetly, as if they were married.

"Yes, we're meeting in my office, would you care to join us?" Ari replied offhandedly.

"Love it. Be right there, darling," Nastassia said blithely.

Flummoxed, Ari stumbled back into his office. Only seconds later Nastassia came through the same door in her street garb, carrying a bucket of champagne and four glasses expertly in her fingers. Ari, still standing, turned around and introduced them.

"Miss Petrova, Mister Wagner," he said sonorously and the two nodded in a genteel fashion to one another.

Nastassia began pouring their glasses, as she intoned, "Charmed."

"Me too," Otto said, beholding her derrière. "I certainly like you better this way, Miss Petrova, than in your bitchy mood of this morning."

She handed them their drinks. "Well, when you get me cornered in an alley, I react like a rat. I must apologize... I don't know what got into me," she said authentically. Drink in hand, she began to move toward the Gothic chair but Ari held her arm gently and offered his own desk seat.

"This is much more comfortable, sweetheart," Ari said, settling into a mental framework of pretending to be married. Nastassia smiled gratefully and took the padded swivel-chair, which was positioned to dominate the room, while Ari sat on the edge of the wooden torture chair.

Otto kept his countenance impassive although inside he wanted to roast Ari alive. *That does it. He has gone over to the other side,* he thought murderously.

Nastassia looked at Ari and moved her hand over to the button, just so he would know that she knew. "To forgiveness," she toasted. They raised their glasses and drank.

"I will forgive you, my dear," Otto said, "but only if you let us know what the hell you're doing here."

Cholmondeley's voice came through the intercom speaker on the desk. "Sir, Miss Moon is here." They all looked at each other.

"Bring her here, Chumley, and bring another chair," Ari said.

Nastassia stood up and poured champagne into the fourth glass, which she had brought into the office when she came in. Cholmondeley brought in a stunningly ornate seventeenth-century French chair, then left to see Seana in.

"Miss Moon?" Nastassia suddenly locked eyes with Ari, feigning jealousy.

"Of Theta Force..." Ari said against his will. Otto saw this eye locking, heard these apparently forced-out words and turned white. Nastassia sat back down at the desk.

"How interesting," she said coolly.

"That's quite a little talent you have there, Miss Petrova," Otto said.

"Thank you, Mister Wagner," Nastassia said charmingly.

"Please... call me 'Otto'."

"Otto," she said, and for a moment all Otto could see was her eyes.

The butler led Seana in. Nastassia handed her a glass and said, "Miss Moon? I'm Miss Petrova—how do you do. I believe you know these gentlemen?" The two ladies clinked glasses, the men joined in, and then all sat down, Ari still perched far forward on the stinging chair—just in case.

"Well, where shall we begin?" Nastassia took over, as if mandated by her position at Ari's desk. "Here's the brief: Seana and I are on opposing American and Russian psychic spy teams, Ari is a good American—he was not good before, but tonight I had my way with him and he has caught goodness—and Otto is a representative of The Leaders, who he says are the originators of *The Message*."

"Thanks for that recap," Seana said. "I thought we'd have to lie to each other until the cows come home."

Nastassia looked back at her, pleased.

"I recognized you," Seana went on in the spirit of full disclosure, "from the UN and before that from my colleague's description of you on the day we all heard *The Message*."

Seana looked at Otto and Ari sympathetically, "Guys, with all due respect, The Leaders you introduced me to aren't the true leaders. They are a faction that split off from the real leaders."

Ari nodded slowly, getting it, then froze as he noted Otto's head swinging around to look at him.

"My dear," Otto said icily, "I am much older than any of you, and I know whereof I speak. Have any of you physically been up on that spaceship hovering above Earth? Do you know who owns it? Do you know its name? You are all very new to the game and you think you know everything. I have seen your type come and go. You don't know how much you don't know. Listen to the voice of experience before you throw your lives away."

"Otto," Seana said enthusiastically, "if you're going to put us in the picture, I'm all for it!"

Otto mustered his dignity. "I'm not going to tell you everything or perhaps anything without first knowing what we are agreeing to in all directions."

They all absorbed Otto's proviso.

Ari, being most experienced in such things, spoke first. "All I want is to be able to live my life in America. I don't care about anything else. I want out from all these dangerous escapades. I'm going to find a farm girl and marry her. That's my latest inspiration."

"Good man," Nastassia encouraged him. "I hear they make perfect mates, very down to earth, attributes all psychics need."

She looked at Otto. "Otto, I don't want to meet your 'Leaders'. I've met the real leaders and I've met lots of false ones. I can tell the difference. There is no deal between us because there is no interest in any deal."

Otto nodded, deciding to capture her somehow and sell her to the Americans or the highest bidder.

"But that doesn't mean I don't wish you the best," she concluded sincerely. They all stared at her.

"My job is to meet the source of *The Message*," Seana said, "like every other psychic investigator on Earth right now. So I know I'm not divulging anything but the obvious, and I know you all know that already. My mind is open to any way we might be able to help each other or at least avoid hurting each other if that's feasible."

Otto seemed to melt a little—for just a second before his face hardened again. "Stay away from Ari and me is all I can say. You all have no idea of who The Leaders are and how much power they have. The further away from us you can stay, the safer you both will be, and that's what I wish you both!"

Ω

Nastassia and Seana walked quickly south and within minutes reached the Waldorf. Along the way they faced off two muggers who somehow knew better than to attack.

In Harry's Bar the attitude was upbeat and lively as always. It could have been the Roaring Twenties with F. Scott Fitzgerald holding court. The ladies sat down and ordered drinks, Nastassia waiting to hear what Seana would order, so both winding up with Stoli on the rocks with a twist.

Nastassia reached across the table to hold Seana's hand. "Sister, we have been together many times for a very long time on this mission," she said affectionately.

"I know," Seana said, wiping back a tear, finding it hard to talk and breathe at the same time. "I knew it when I saw you." They sat quietly for a minute or two.

"What do you know about the mission? Are there five of us?" Seana asked finally.

"I think that feels about right," Nastassia said unsurely. "I recognize you for sure. Another I know for sure is my love, a man, a warrior. There are others too I sense... "

"What is our mission?"

"I wish I knew."

They sat in silence. The waiter came and they ordered another round.

They held up their glasses. "Let's pray we can know our mission soon," Seana said, and Nastassia nodded and clinked.

"I sensed what Ari had done to you and I did it back to him," Nastassia confessed.

Seana almost splurted out a mouthful of champagne with a laugh.

"I know I taught him a lesson. He might become a better person," Nastassia added modestly.

"You might be wondering how he got me in that position," Seana offered, wanting not to be seen as a loose woman by this sister from the ages.

Nastassia nodded, alert for any information that could get her out of the fix of having to either succeed in connecting the Russians to someone they believed to be the source of *The Message*, or to face frightening consequences for failure to do so. But she did not want to help people like Otto amass stronger gangs.

"Ari said that going through Otto was the only way he had found to be able to connect other people to The Leaders, which was—and still is—our assignment, same as yours," Seana started.

"Who else had he connected?" Nastassia put in.

"Apparently women he had bedded. One night stands mostly, he said. Some were paid prostitutes," Seana recounted from their conversations earlier that confusing and frightening night.

"Did he know if they remained connected after the one sexual liaison?" Nastassia pressed her, always one step ahead.

"I asked him that," Seana said, pleased with herself for thinking of it too. "He said that he met up with some of those women again and found them to be much more elevated in their thinking, in more powerful roles professionally, doing a lot of global travel, a lot happier and far more confident— none of which sounded appealing to me of course but I pretended that it did. Ari thinks of me as having low self-esteem so I have been playing that part for him."

"So some kind of permanent connection, it would appear," Nastassia mused. "But despite how these women look and act on the outside, how can we know what their inner lives are like? Could it be that they have been completely taken over by these—beings—?"

"As in demonic possession, you're thinking," Seana said.

Nastassia nodded and added, "Who knows how long these 'Leaders' have been at their game?"

14

"Otto, put that away," Ari said, eyeing the gun.

"Okay," Otto said, and tucked the gun in his leather small-of-back holster. "But you are acting contrary to the interests of The Leaders. As your friend, I'm going to try to talk you down from the ceiling. If that doesn't work, my gun is the least of your problems."

"I'm all ears."

"This planet needs The Leaders to be in charge of all the world's governments—that's the big secret," Otto disclosed.

"I know how poorly our governments are run right now, so keep talking," Ari chimed in. "Why would their running things be guaranteed to make things any better?"

"They're smarter and more experienced—their culture is much older," Otto replied.

"The human race would be taking a big chance," Ari mused. "Things aren't really so bad the way they are."

Otto had run out of things to say. He didn't want to kill Ari. Ari's businesses allowed him to launder the cash from his stolen art deals. It would be a huge inconvenience to have to set someone else up to fill that role. The art had been stolen from the Jews a long time ago, and its documentation made it almost impossible to fence. Ari had bought a lot of it and that was the first time any of it had moved in Otto's lifetime.

"Get high or die," Otto said, riffing in the hope of accidentally stumbling upon a compelling case. "There are many of us down here in human bodies working toward that end."

"Are you saying you're not human, Otto?"

"No, I am human, but I have seen them—the non-humans— The Leaders." Otto said passionately.

"Otto, I can't believe this—you're telling me you've seen extraterrestrials?!"

"Yes. Many times. As will you, very soon. Don't bail."

Ari leaned forward. "Tell me more."

"I was not even born when this plan was drafted, but I was there at the conference in Madrid."

Ari heard a sound of distant thunder. He saw a flash of eagle-topped fluted columns.

"The Plan requires that there be complete demoralization." Otto locked eyes with Ari.

"Remember the two Kennedy assassinations? And Lee Harvey Oswald? Martin Luther King? Marilyn Monroe? John Lennon? Princess Diana? The World Trade Towers? The stock market crashes of 1987 and 2008? The space shuttle explosion? The January 6 insurrection?"

Ari sat there speechless, taking it all in, thinking to himself, *This madman talking like this about all these dead people, all the losses suffered. Who is this guy?*

"I can tell this man needs a little more convincing," a booming voice proclaimed as a giant man came through the door.

Ari looked up, wondering how tall the man must be to need to stoop in his nine-foot ceilinged office. *Extraterrestrial?* The thought shot through his mind and blew it, instantly erasing a lifetime of half-hearted superficial disciplining of himself. He became servile and stood up unsteadily to shake hands, flinching as he saw the alien's face clearly. It looked exactly like the face of Adolf Hitler.

In his mind Ari heard himself screaming hysterically. His blood turned to ice and his ability to think turned to mush. He was very young when he first heard the stories from his grandparents, who were among only 144 prisoners who had escaped in the history of Auschwitz. His other relatives of that era were among the million who perished there. He wanted to run but was too afraid to make any move.

This huge Hitler doppelganger looked down at Ari as if he were a slimy little snail caught outside its shell, his disgust and hate pouring down like warped sunlight from his eyes, contempt from his snarling smile.

At the same time, Perse's other apparent human body, this one normal sized, was in Iran leading a revolution to take over the country by psychic subterfuge. Perse had no trouble paying a decent amount of attention to his two selves, and could even go to three if he so chose. Being the Second Son—or avatar—of the One Self, he was the third most powerful entity in the multiverse.

"You stinking little Jew," Hitler spat at Ari. "This is the gratitude you show for the way I have transformed your life, and even your own being—your ability to fight, becoming wildly rich, having women ten times a week. You do remember how it was before, don't you?"

"I'm so sorry—" Ari said in a begging voice, which he had rarely heard come out of himself other than recently with Nastassia. However, now he also heard the terror in his own voice, much more uncontrolled fear than he thought he was capable of. His will felt completely broken.

"My servant here," Hitler indicated Otto, who looked up lovingly, grateful to be mentioned in even this demeaning way by his idol.

Like many others, discovering that *der Führer* was not dead had been the most exhilarating moment of Otto's life. Then being selected to serve *Him*—now revealed to have been not only the superhuman Hitler but also the oldest of the *Armanen*, the original Titans who preceded even the gods—made Otto happy and fulfilled in a way that nothing else on Earth could ever have achieved, or so he thought.

"Was it so much that he asked you," Hitler went on, "to let the little lady sit in the chair and get pricked? If I can't depend on you, you shall have to endure eternal suffering." He started to make his hands metaphorically weigh things in one hand then the other. "Eternal suffering, depend on you, hmm..."

Ari couldn't believe what he did next. Some survival mechanism caused him to go down on his knees at Hitler's feet and hug his ankles, which made him feel utterly despicable. Tears flowed down his face.

"Please, *mein Führer*, forgive my error! How could I have known—until I saw you for myself in all your glory—" Ari remembered his survivor grandparents and gagged a bit on the last word.

Hitler petted his head like a dog's.

"Please! Just tell me what you want of me."

"Okay, Mr. Brain, then up and at 'em! One more transgression and it's the Inner Circle of the Lake of Hell for you. What I want is to be connected to all those who want to meet The Leaders, or to the source of *The Message*, and you are my ambassador," Hitler said, then disappeared as if he had too many other things to do to even say goodbye, or perhaps because they were both so unimportant and he had already spent too much time with them.

More than anything else that he had seen up to that point, Ari was awestruck that Hitler was able to just disappear. He couldn't think of a word to say or what to do next. He sat on the floor dumbfounded.

Otto looked at him enviously.

Ω

"Nastassia is never going to defect, they have her parents," Seana was saying. The three of them were alone in the conference room. "She is friendly toward me because of our past lives working together, but she can't stay in touch without endangering herself and her parents."

"Sounds like The Leaders *want* to establish connections, maybe that was even what was behind their transmission," Shannon mused, shifting gears after having heard Seana's full report.

"Tim, let's not assume that it was The Leaders who made the transmission," Marty reminded him, and Shannon nodded.

"Either it's them who want to make the connections, or Ari is using his relationship with them as a snare for women," Seana hypothesized. "I got the feeling from my conversation with the Captain—or whoever he is, that he likes having sex with us Earth natives, he finds our innocence attractive." She laughed, suddenly remembering something she had forgotten from the apparently lifelike dream. "He said that the women down here are nicer people than the ones on the ship."

"So which way do we think it is," Marty asked, "that this sex connection bit is just the mid-level troops having a little fun, or is it the head of the expedition, or the governance above him, who has mandated it?"

Everyone shook their heads, none venturing a guess.

"What will be the effect of allowing this to go on?" Shannon asked, thinking out loud. "Will these women be part of an invasion?"

"Sounds like we have a lot to lose and nothing to gain by allowing this creeping infiltration to continue," Seana said. "How do we stop it?"

"Ari's a citizen," Shannon said. "We can't regulate his sex life, we can't liquidate him or hurt him in any way or constrain his freedom. I don't see how under these conditions we can stop this trickle of apparent landings..."

"Let's track down some of the women 'victims' and see if we can learn anything from them," Marty suggested, and the other two nodded.

Ω

Ari stopped cage fighting and ended his lessons with Dr. Chi. He cancelled his mercs, paying them a cancellation fee that would keep them at his disposal if needed. The one thing he knew for certain was that he belonged to Hitler, who must be the Devil, and that he had no way out, no hope. He must do only what Hitler—or his emissary Otto—told him to do. Draw women to his bed and serve as a conduit to whoever on board the ship would be having sex with them through him—he'd become the Devil's pimp.

What have I ever done to deserve this? Is this my real comeuppance for what I put Seana through? I thought Nastassia's lesson was more than enough. This now seems to be an overreaction on God's part—if there even is a God. Perhaps the Devil owns the universe...

In order to make Hitler happy, Ari knew he had to keep going to one or another of his now giant chain of fight clubs every night, or to some other meat wagons, where he could pick up a hooker or a civilian to bring home and bed. His destiny now, as he saw it. He could think of worse jobs, but not worse bosses. He hoped he could maintain erection now that he had seen his own petty value in Hitler's eyes. *Stay hard or die,* he laughed to himself sardonically.

He sat at the top table in the tiered large ballroom surrounding the main fighting ring, the only tier above the ring level. With no one fighting right now, the main event being over, people milled around, meeting each other, drinking, and getting stoned. Given his fame and good looks, he never had to sit alone for long before some woman would approach and ask to join him. He looked idly around, seeing if he saw anyone that he might like—he could always send someone to fetch her.

God, he prayed, *if you would appear to me like Hitler did, it would help me a lot.*

Some Jew, he thought. *Some faith, requiring God to appear to help me do the Devil's bidding. Perhaps that's it— maybe this is a test of my faith.*

So far, he judged himself to be failing miserably. *What do I expect after a lifetime of faking being a Jew?*

As if in a spotlight, he saw Nastassia's face across the room, just entering. She spotted him right away and began to climb the stairs. In a minute she was by his side and slid onto the banquette next to him.

"Friends?" she asked, meaning to be clear that sex was still out of the picture.

"Yes, of course. Great to see a friend," Ari said genuinely. "What will you have?" A waitress stood nearby, several in fact hovering to do his bidding. They ordered Stoli on the rocks.

"How is life?" Nastassia asked.

"Something's missing—might be you—" Ari didn't know where to begin or what would be unwise to say, not sure who might be listening.

She blushed becomingly. "Nice of you to say, after those dirty tricks I played on you," she said with a soft laugh.

"I knew you did it because I needed it done," Ari admitted. "I have to thank you for waking me up. I had not been thinking or feeling clearly until then. You made a *mensch* out of me." *Just in time for hell,* he thought.

She had to read his mind to decode "*mensch*" and coincidentally picked up the word "hell".

"I take it you have fallen into some rough times... Care to talk about it?" she asked, sounding to herself a little prying and manipulative, and so about to take it back.

"No," he said. "I can't, sorry. But enough about me—how are you coming with your mission?"

"That's why I'm here, actually." she said candidly. "My bosses have someone they want to meet The Leaders."

"That's exciting," he said, seeing some possible bonanza in the situation for himself, connecting Hitler and the Russians. *Probably could be shot for treason,* he realized, though sure that what Hitler would do to him would be far worse if he declined. *For a while it might make me feel like my old self again, to be parleying with Hitler and Russia and who knows who else. Better than being focused on pimping.*

"But not you," he said questioningly.

She looked at him affectionately. "As you know," she replied.

"So they must treat you pretty well to let you off the hook and replace you with another agent. I had quite a different image of conditions in the country of my birth," Ari fished.

"Not at all, they are horrendous not only to me but in general. Fortunately, I was able to scare the pants off them, and they didn't want to risk me," Nastassia confided.

"How did you scare them?"

"They see me as promising and they don't want to lose me. I could be their strongest psychic," Nastassia said, feeling immodest.

She went on, "I told them that connecting with psychic beings sexually or in any other profound way could open the door to mental takeover, which they had never thought about. One of them, my immediate boss, who is on the edge of hitting me whenever I say anything that sounds spiritual, said 'Then what you are saying my dear'"—she imitated Karesky's puffed-up style, which made Ari smile and feel relaxed for the first time in days—"'is that what spiritualists thought of as demonic possession could have been actually these extraterrestrials taking over human minds.' He loved the idea that his pupil was finally giving scientific explanations to things instead of superstitious ones."

"So who is this other woman, is she going to be here tonight?" Ari asked, beginning by their closeness to feel normally horny again. He didn't know what perfume she wore but he was totally seduced by it, and stared down her cleavage without shame. Then he smiled a brotherly smile and clasped her hand. "Thanks for being a friend, Nastassia," he said.

"Always," she promised sincerely. Nastassia wanted to always be everyone's friend. "And no, she won't be in the States until tomorrow but they wanted me to clear the way with you. They will get in touch."

He looked briefly upset at not being offered a specific meeting time and place, and would have to wonder when would they show up. Then he remembered he was no longer the boss who could call the shots, and he had best keep his head down and follow orders until he figured out a better plan.

"By the way, what is that perfume you're wearing?"

"Joy," she answered, smiling.

Just then, Khan and Jason arrived and joined them. Ari rose uncertainly. He hadn't seen them since before his meeting with Hitler. Now he knew them to be Hitler's enemy—recalling what they had said about Otto being a rogue, from some split-off faction of The Leaders—which put him in great danger by their presence. Standing reflexively, he began to hold out his hand then visibly retracted it.

"Hi, I'm Nastassia. Who are you?" she asked the two arrivals.

They knew who she was, of course, and she pretended to not know Jason to keep from getting him in any further trouble. She figured his following her had not been in his orders.

"I'm Jason Page," he said and took her hand, kissing it.

Khan shook hands with her, liking her strong grip. "Khan," he said, "at your service."

"These are the true leaders," Nastassia whispered to Ari, hoping that only the four of them could hear her.

"I have joined the other side," Ari announced a bit coldly and quite matter-of-factly so as to leave no room to brook conversation about it. "The die is cast. Right or wrong, I have made my final decision."

"Can we at least talk about it?" Khan asked.

Ari's fear level mounted suddenly as he sensed Hitler watching all this. He conveyed his apology to Nastassia with his eyes and bolted for the door. No one followed him.

15

"One of them is now on the president's staff as an intern," Seana reported. "When Ari met her, she was a manicurist. She had come to give him a pedicure. Another who was a junior writer for a small magazine now has a powerful editorial position at a publishing company Ari owns. The whole pattern is like that. These attractive but not otherwise extraordinary women are getting career boosts beyond their wildest dreams."

"That doesn't tell us anything about them on the inside," Marty said. "Are they better people than they were before, do they have the same sense of self, or is it just that Mr. Brain can afford to hire them or do a payola to get them hired?"

"I spoke to four of them," Seana reported, "and each one sounded highly intelligent and driven. Of course I never knew them before, so they may have always been that way. But it does seem unusual that four out of four are now on par with Type A CEOs."

"Does Ari go for brainy hard-driving types?" Marty asked.

Seana laughed and shook her head. "I think he prefers the weaker type—classic submissive and adoring women," Seana answered carefully, "but I can't say for sure."

"So The Leaders are changing these women—" Shannon started.

"Either by mental takeover, or some other way," Marty concluded.

Shannon's cellphone sounded its Star-Spangled Banner ringtone and he quickly took the call. "Okay, send it in here and everybody come," Shannon said and clicked off. "Some action at Nastassia's suite, coming on our screen now—"

First they heard the sound of people talking and then they saw the image as if from a great distance, a video lens perched near the high ceiling. Nastassia welcomed some burly-looking men into her suite. They spoke in Russian. The whole New York Theta Team, as if there in the room, watched and listened. Nastassia hurriedly threw her things together and left with the men. She seemed to be perfectly at ease, not a captive.

"What does this mean?" Jason asked, clearly concerned for his unrequited beloved.

"Probably heading for the airport and back to Russia, I'd say," Seana opined.

"Mission accomplished then?" Shannon asked. "They connected with The Leaders?"

"It would seem so," Marty said. "She may not have been involved in the actual connection, but it comes to the same thing."

"They could have had other operatives—" Khan conjectured.

"It couldn't have taken the Russians long to find a woman Ari would bed," Donna suggested, and most nodded. "A simple enough solution in the end," she added.

Ω

Nastassia watched alone from the back of the black stretch limo as it moved slowly up Park Avenue, followed by its twin. The two large tough-looking men up front whom she knew to be GRU Spetsnaz were on the lookout for someone on the street. She came into view, standing out like a bright light—a beautiful leggy blonde in a yellow dress, with a million-dollar smile. The guard helped her into the back seat with Nastassia, who held out her hand.

"Nastassia," she said. "Welcome sister."

"Kaitanya Astrolova," the blonde replied in a rich aristo-cratic Russian accent. They shook hands. "I understand I'm replacing you in this assignment. They didn't tell me much."

"They never do. In short, Ari didn't like me," Nastassia lied, "but I'm sure he will go wild over you."

Kaitanya liked all that very much and quickly dropped her guard with Nastassia. "Yes, men seem to," she said.

Nastassia guessed her to be in her late twenties, or maybe older.

"What does he especially like?" Kaitanya asked.

Nastassia blushed. She was normally very prim when talk-ing about such things and sensed Kaitanya to be a worldly woman. "Bondage, I guess," she finally said, unable to think of anything else to say.

"How good is he telepathically?" Kaitanya asked.

Nastassia realized the essential purpose of Kaitanya join-ing her on this limo trip: for Kaitanya to learn as much as she could from her. They had just made a U-turn, now heading south on Park Avenue and going slower than traffic, so clearly they had no particular destination.

"He's not half bad at reading, not very good at protecting his own mind," Nastassia said.

"Amateur then?"

"The Leaders have been training him. That's how he is able to connect us to them," Nastassia disclosed. She then touched Kaitanya's leg like a confidante. "Sister, don't turn your back on these so-called Leaders. I don't trust them. Connect to them but don't let your mind be taken over."

Kaitanya looked frightened. She had not been expecting this potential risk.

"I'm sure you will be fine," Nastassia reassured her. "I'm only telling you to help you, not to scare you—you have what it takes to stay in control."

The words "bondage" and "control" connected in her mind and Kaitanya began to internally rehearse who she would be to this man, the connector, Ari.

Nastassia saw Kaitanya's expression turning into a dominatrix, as she assuredly put on that role like clothing. Nastassia
thought she looked really gorgeous that way. She tried on the
same expression, for fun.

"What's your rank, Kaitanya?" Nastassia asked idly, wanting to begin to get closer.

"Colonel," Kaitanya responded, "and I know you're Lieutenant, but let's forget that stuff, we're just girls, okay?"

They hugged, and Nastassia felt delighted. She had never
had a friend at Psycho and it was too cold an environment for
her warm-hearted instincts. She hoped they would be able to
stay in contact when they got back to Russia.

They told each other their life stories. Nastassia's father, the
Russian ambassador to Cuba, met her Chinese-Cuban mother
in Cuba. After her birth they returned to Russia. Her parents
had noticed she had strange powers as a small child and they
had tried to conceal these abilities and dissuade her from using
them. Nevertheless, other children could see that Nastassia
had unusual insights and told their parents about her. As she
grew up, the powers became self-starting. She had many Flow
state experiences of her body and mind doing their own thing,
herself a spectator. The eventual showdown had come when
Psycho arrived and insisted she must join their team. She cou-
rageously refused, then collapsed when they took her parents
hostage to force her compliance.

Nastassia wiped away a tear as she finished telling her
story, adding, "They still have my parents."

Kaitanya hugged Nastassia and then began telling her
story. She was born in Shanghai, where her Russian family had been one of the prominent families for decades. Her
father was an artificial intelligence (AI) genius and entrepre-
neur whose companies operated globally. Her Chinese mother
was a singer, a chanteuse, and that's what Kaitanya aspired to
be when she grew up. Her story then became similar to Nastassia's—being discovered by Psycho and forcefully recruited,
using threats against her family as their tool of choice.

"How did they discover you are a psychic?' Nastassia asked, compassionately.

"All the AI journals wrote up that a human being had been found to have the ability to read the mind of an AI," Kaitanya replied, "I was about your age when it happened. You're about nineteen, yes?"

Nastassia nodded and smiled ever so slightly, hating to lie, especially to her dear new wonderful friend, but not wanting to admit she was so very young. They had so much in common! Chinese on their mother's side, psychics, trapped into Psycho, parents threatened. Nastassia imagined them walking casually down the halls in the Psycho headquarters side by side, smiling and laughing.

Ω

"I'm still thinking about it," the Danang Lama said affectionately. He sat in lotus position on a comfortable pillow on a velvet-upholstered bench, looking out a huge viewport at the Earth hanging large in front of him, in a state of bliss. But then, that's where he lived.

His visitor, a handsome man in a military uniform, had movie-star hair and a smile to match. "And what are your thoughts, sir?" the visitor asked politely. He had introduced himself as Perse and said this was his spaceship, his democratic empire.

When they helped him escape after the assassination attempt at the UN, they had explained that their civilization, which covered all of the galaxies in the universe, had been watching Earthlings for millions of years and helping them along.

The Lama was delighted at meeting extraterrestrials and being in their spacecraft. He had been thrilled at the ride up in the speedy smaller spacecraft. They treated him respectfully and told him that The Message had come from them, that it was their first step in making themselves known to humankind.

One of them had informed him, "We identified you as the most advanced of your species and so selected you to become our ambassador. And while we had planned to meet you in a more pleasant way, we swooped in when we saw you in danger."

"You haven't told me the complete plan," the Lama said reasonably.

"We represent no danger to Earth," Perse said. "We have saved you many times as a species." He chuckled, then added suavely, "Your species seems to have a death wish."

The Lama smiled at the attempt at humor although he secretly found it in bad taste. He waited for more disclosure of Perse's long-term plans for Earth. All Perse had divulged so far was his view that the race now deserved to be brought into cosmic civilization, and that the Lama would play an ongoing role in the spiritual governance of the planet.

"I sense that you don't trust me," Perse said, looking suddenly like a young man whose feelings have been hurt.

The Lama felt instant compassion for him, as was Perse's intent.

"Have I given you any reason to distrust me?" he asked miserably, with seeming authenticity.

"Two reasons," the Lama announced without hesitation. "You maintain a strong mind shield at all times, and you appear to be holding back details."

"Fair points," Perse allowed. "In our civilization it is one of our highest ethical standards not to intrude into each other's minds. And there is no fixed plan... we open up ourselves to a newly accepted planet and see what happens."

"You obviously have some intention of sharing in the governance of the planet, if you can offer me a role in spiritual governance—?" the Lama said inquisitively, with a rising inflection.

"You are already performing as a spiritual governor for Earth, sir," Perse said, as if slightly miffed.

"And your role in planetary governance?" the Lama asked the direct question.

"To be determined, by your people and mine, democratically," Perse insisted, continuing his subterfuge.

The Lama paused. "That gives me a lot of food for thought, Perse," he said graciously.

"Take all the time you need," Perse said, rising respectfully.

"While I'm thinking," the Lama added gently, "if you would be so kind as to put it in writing...?"

"Of course," Perse said with inner glee. He loved making these contracts with humans. *They think they're so smart,* he thought to himself. He was having a good time now.

Ω

The six New York based Theta agents entered the enormous Quonset hut and looked up at the ship whose name they'd been told was Behemoth. It certainly merited the name. The giant dirigible looked exactly like the ones they were used to seeing over New York, with GOODYEAR on its side in gigantic letters. They knew, however, that this blimp was much larger and very differently equipped. Captain Miller stood there to greet them and hustled them aboard. He reminded them not to touch the outer skin of the ship, as it was slightly radioactive—a side effect of the radar-defying stealth tech.

Ground crews removed the cables and helped trundle the ship out of its hangar at JFK— off in a corner of the airport and pointing away from the main terminal, so the ship's movement would be unnoticed. It was night anyway and their take-off almost soundless as they drifted slowly upward, soon out of the traffic patterns of the airport.

It had been Williams who said they would need to commandeer this secret ship, which specialized in spy operations around the Northeast and was used by all the intelligence agencies on a first-call basis. Fortunately it had not been in use when Theta called.

No one knew why Williams was right about this, including Williams. But they trusted his intuition now that he had been so clearly in the Flow state for days on end.

The ship took up station very high up over Manhattan and far from the usual air lanes. Their contact at Air Traffic Control kept in constant touch with them as Behemoth would be invisible to planes and helicopters.

Through the powerful telephoto lenses they were able to see Cholmondeley walking out on the terrace to clear away champagne glasses.

Ω

Cholmondeley showed Kaitanya in and introduced her to Ari. Wearing an amber bathrobe with matching slippers, Ari was in an uncharacteristically subdued mood, yet his eyes widened and his face returned a bit of its cockiness as he took in Kaitanya's intoxicating beauty. She had it turned up full. Her eyes, cheekbones, and lips formed a divine harmony to his eye. They shook hands, and after a moment's hesitation Ari kissed her hand.

"Miss Kaitanya Astrolova, of the Russian embassy," Cholmondeley announced. "Mr. Ari Mann."

"Good to meet you, Miss Astrolova," Ari started as his butler bowed out.

"Call me Kaitanya, please," she said, emoting the air of a dominatrix, which he noticed and found arousing.

He led her into the living room, where they sat on a sofa together. In front of them were two buckets of ice, one containing a bottle of Stolichnaya Cristall, the other a bottle of Dom Perignon. She nodded at the Stoli.

"Ice?" he asked and she shook her head. He took the Stoli too, the same way, and clinked glasses with her.

"To us," he said.

"And to meeting The Leaders," she added. They sipped.

"Did they tell you the protocol for meeting The Leaders?" he asked.

She smiled dominatingly, but not unsweetly. "Oh yes, I understand that we are to enjoy sexual congress and this very enjoyment will draw them into a mental connection with me."

Intrigued with the way the process had been described to her, he thought to himself, *Yes, that is not inaccurate.*

"More than that, though," Ari added. "You will have the experience of sex with them, with The Leaders themselves."

She had supposed as much. "With one of them, or many of them—?"

He shook his head.

"And then, when I return to Russia, will I still be able to stay in contact with them?"

"I don't know, Kaitanya," Ari admitted humbly, "I've never done anything exactly like this before. They speak to me in my mind all the time, giving me advice... I hope that you experience that too... forever..." He realized that he was being honest with her even though it might mean they could wind up not having sex together. He was amazed at himself, but not disapproving.

"We're going to do this my way, you understand," Kaitanya said unequivocally, and he nodded sheepishly.

"I promise," he said sincerely. He would never take a woman by force or deceit again. He was beginning to respect women as equals. These changes astonished him.

"Where shall we do it?" Kaitanya asked in a businesslike manner.

I wonder if she's a professional prostitute, Ari thought to himself.

"Come, let me show you my bedroom," he bade her, and they both stood, bringing their glasses, although Ari knew there was another set-up in the bedroom. He led the way, with Kaitanya delighting in the art and statues adorning the walls and hallways.

They reached his bedroom and she wordlessly expressed her approval of his furnishings. Stargazer lilies had been set up all around, filling the room with their sweet fragrance.

"Take off your clothes," she commanded, and Ari put down his glass and obeyed.

"Now kiss me," she said, setting down her glass.

He slowly moved closer, smiling happily, ready to receive his reward for being a good boy. He put his arms around her and kissed her gently though passionately—already extremely aroused given the recent ultimately unsatisfying events with Seana and Nastassia. Their lips parted and she smiled at him.

"Good," she said. Stepping away from him, she took off her clothes and lied down on the bed, facing him. He stood awaiting orders, knowing she expected this of him.

"I want your face here," she said, pointing at her labia, which were opening like a moist pink lotus. He readily obeyed. For most of an hour he continued to follow the orders she gave, while she herself remained totally passive, although encouraging. She had taken the pill and so was not distressed when Ari had an orgasm inside of her, though mildly surprised to hear him cry out, "Nastassia!" His orgasm went on a long time and then he appeared to fall asleep on top of her. She lied still, closed her eyes and waited.

16

The air felt somehow different, colder and no longer smell-ing fragrant. She opened her eyes to find a different man on top of her, in a setting that appeared to be a spacecraft. The man lifted his head slowly and looked at her from inches away. Perse had put away his Hitler face and now wore the debonair and handsome face he knew she would want to see. Indeed, her face lit up with excitement.

"My Leader," she said reverentially. Perse merely smiled and began making love to her without a word. She let herself enjoy it, taking a far more active role than she had with Ari, which Perse appreciated. He knew she was auditioning for a permanent relationship and he let himself be convinced she would be worth staying in touch with. Besides, he'd planned the whole thing just this way.

Hours later they stopped to enjoy some afterglow. To amuse her, Perse blew smoke rings, without having to smoke anything. She laughed and then had the ludicrous thought that maybe she was in bed with the very Devil.

"What happens now?" Kaitanya asked innocently.

Perse smiled at her. "I'm going to send you back down to Earth, but we will stay in touch," he said, touching her inti-mately.

"Can I call you in my mind whenever I want to?" Kaitanya asked.

"Well, you know, I'm a very busy man..." Perse began, toying with her.

She pouted gorgeously. He chuckled.

"Don't worry, if you need me, I'll be there," he lied. "Besides I'm going to give you a Guardian Angel," he added.

She immediately pictured another man, a Leader, who would stay with her on Earth, and wondered if he would be as good looking and well-endowed.

"Oh, that's exciting," she said, grateful. Her bosses would be pleased to have their very own Leader right there with them. This could get her promoted to General. Her bosom expanded with pride.

"Come, let's meet your Guardian Angel," Perse said, taking her hand and stepping off the bed. She dutifully followed and then stopped. He turned and she pointed at their nudity.

"Is this a way to meet people?" she wondered. Perse laughed a bit boisterously.

"You're here in your astral body my dear—your physical body is down on Park Avenue—so you can make your body appear anyway you like right now," Perse said, making his hair grow long to demonstrate.

He opened the door to the adjacent cabin, and she walked through, experimenting with body "illusioning". She gave herself multicolored ever-changing tattoos and admired them crisscrossing her body in waves. When she looked up, she found herself in a lounge with a transparent wall, where the Earth hung straight outside. In front of her stood an imposing female in a military uniform who didn't look to be human, with strange but beautiful ears that curved up into her hair, big gorgeous eyes, and very long eyelashes. She looked tough and strong, not like an Angel, her expression confident and in control.

"Kaitanya, meet Goma. Goma, Kaitanya," Perse said.

The ladies shook hands. Goma's handshake hurt Kaitanya's hand but she didn't show it.

The next thing Kaitanya knew, she was back on Ari's bed and his body was still asleep on top of her. She had a sudden notion that Ari must have been put to sleep by The Leaders. She looked around the room but didn't see Goma. *Where is my Guardian Angel?*

I'm right here, Goma's voice said in her mind.

Ω

Nastassia scooted over as Kaitanya got into the car. She had become concerned after many hours of waiting and wondered if she would ever see her friend again.

"I'm so glad you're all right," Nastassia said and moved to hug her.

Kaitanya wanted to hug back but felt her body stiffen and give a cold response, and she had no control over it. In sudden terror she realized that Goma had taken her over completely.

Nastassia sat back quickly, noting the other's coldness. "Sorry, Colonel," she apologized formally, and Kaitanya nodded curtly, mostly ignoring her. Nastassia felt heartbroken.

A GRU Spetsnaz officer opened the door and invited Ari to enter. He had been taken at gunpoint and he knew those guns although concealed were still pointed at him. Unsure of who these people were or what side they were on or which sides even existed, Ari wasn't sure who he himself was anymore. He didn't let himself worry. Whoever these people were, at least they didn't seem to want him dead. Maybe this was leading to a better situation. Maybe not. He had no idea of his chances one way or another. Despite his prowess as a fighter, he knew these men to be well-armed and well-trained professional murderers and they outnumbered him at least six to one—he couldn't see how many were in the second car.

They seated him between the two ladies, which immediately improved his mood. Kaitanya now ignored him contemptuously. He shared a glance with Nastassia as if to ask, "What's with her?" but Nastassia merely shrugged and made a "Who knows?" face. The officer got in, closing the door, and stretched out on the long leather couch facing Ari and the ladies, his gun now in plain sight in the dark-windowed limo, pointed at Ari.

The two limos moved off, heading north on Park Avenue. Ari went to put his arm around Kaitanya, pursing his lips to say something into her ear, but earned an elbow in the solar plexus which took all the wind out of him for several minutes. This gave him time to think about things in new ways. He hoped they had not hurt Cholmondeley and that the man was all right. *He is a good man. A better man than I,* he thought.

Two police cars suddenly appeared with sirens and lights blazing, coming from two different directions to cut off the two limos. Two more police cars trapped the limos in from behind. Cops with guns drawn, some of them submachineguns, leaped out and surrounded the two cars. The Spetsnaz had been given orders not to create an international incident and in a situation like this they were to surrender without violence. The cops came up to the cars, screaming orders and banging on the windows. The Spetsnaz in both cars got out and put their hands on their heads after throwing their weapons onto the street. Ari got out next and helped the ladies out.

Nastassia didn't know whether to be elated or horrified, as she didn't know where this was going to lead. American prison? Freedom? What about her parents? *This is not my fault, perhaps they won't be punished,* she told herself.

There seemed to Nastassia to be two dozen cops on the scene. They were younger and in better shape than most cops she had seen in New York. Quite a few of them appeared to be totally bald on the parts of their heads not covered by their hats. A contingent of them ushered the three of them to a waiting police car and squeezed them in the back, pushing down on their heads as they helped them in. That police car and another then escorted them from the scene, which had turned into a two-mile parking lot of cars and taxis, unable to move, all the way down to Twenty-third Street.

"Thank you, officers," Ari said to the two cops up front. "What happens now? Going to headquarters to question us?"

"Yes, but not to the public headquarters. There's been a bomb threat—these people are determined to get you, sir," the driver said, eyes on the road. "You're being taken care of under the Witness Protection Act; we're taking you to a safe haven," he added in a protective idealistic voice.

Ω

Cholmondeley was pouring himself some of the boss's best single malt when Ari walked in.

"Sir! You're all right!" he exclaimed and went up to hug him but stopped short.

Ari looked down briefly at the scotch in his butler's hand and Cholmondeley reddened. "No worries," Ari said, "you deserve it. Did they hurt you?"

"Just my pride, sir. I am humiliated that I was unable to protect you," the butler said sincerely.

"I know, I know." Ari said, walking through his apartment with Cholmondeley in tow. "You're a fine man, Chumley. I don't deserve you."

The butler felt weirded out by Ari's behavior. This felt nothing like the Ari he knew so well. Could the young man have really changed so much overnight?

Ari poured himself a drink from the same bottle and waved to indicate they should sit together, which was unheard of. Cholmondeley tried to keep his expression normal, forcing his eyes to pop back into their sockets.

"Chumley," Ari spoke, "you've seen what I've been doing lately."

The butler didn't quite know how to say it. "Yes, sir," he said vaguely, thinking to himself that Ari had been acting like a sex maniac. He had always had at least two or three women a week, but not more than one each day until the last week or so. Cholmondeley had also noticed a change in the women—they were always nicer to *him* coming in than going out. A butler notices such things.

"It may be a mental disorder," Ari admitted, "but for now I'm going to ask that you play along with me on this at least for a little while longer. I'm searching for something—I can't put it into words—and I need your help."

"My help, sir?" The butler knew that a powerful rich man like Ari couldn't possibly need his help.

"Yes," Ari said. "I want to continue my sexual vision quest, but with meaning. I want you to bring me women who are involved in international diplomacy, and each one from a different nation. But no Americans."

"Yes, sir," he said, crushed at being asked to be a pimp now. "Did you say no Americans, sir?" Cholmondeley was dazed by this. Ari loved America.

Perse thought, *I'll never get the Americans, I've given up trying.*

"Three a day please, Chumley, morning, afternoon, and evening," Ari added, ignoring the question except for a head nod of confirmation.

Cholmondeley dared to take a good look at his master. *Who is this person?* He heard his mind ask itself. *Well, of course it must be Mr. Mann, but he's certainly been changed by something. What turned him off America so suddenly?*

Ω

The Danang Lama stood looking out at the beautiful Earth turning slowly in front of him. It was breathtaking, though he breathed consciously, very deeply and slowly, in and out.

Perse had not visited him in more than twenty-four hours, which had not been the former pattern. He wondered what mischief that being had gotten into. He knew Perse's real identity, although Perse had not recognized him. It took the Lama's utmost concentration to fool him, and in time Perse would get it, so time was not on his side.

He walked to the door and touched it, but it didn't open. It had opened to Perse's touch. So the Lama reached his mind into the door and its electronics. The door opened. He stepped out. The door closed behind him.

He found himself on a mezzanine surrounding a huge park with a lake, gardens, a zoo, rides for children, and an enormous skylight above glittering with stars. A band was playing and people were eating, drinking, singing, boating, dancing,

playing, and lying around. Most of them wore military uniforms, some black, and some red. As people passed him on the
ramp, he could see they were of many different species. The red
uniforms had an insignia of a lightning bolt splitting a planet.
The black uniforms had an abstract space battle insignia. *The
Army and Navy,* the Lama thought.

He saw a sweeping down-ramp leading into the park, and
he walked down it, taking in everything in fine detail. Here the
woodsy smell of being on Earth permeated the vast space and
he reveled in the scents he had missed since coming aboard.

The ramp landed him at the zoo, where he saw no children, and only a few species of animals, with bonobos being
the main attraction. The off-duty sailors and soldiers grouped
around the bonobos, watching them endlessly mating, switching partners now and then.

What a loving species, the Lama thought. He was about
to head for the lake when a statuesque female soldier accosted
him, apparently attracted to him sexually, perhaps turned on
by watching the bonobos.

"Hey sonny, want to trade up from your hand?" she asked
him loudly, and the crowd instantly changed the direction of
its attention to gather around them.

"I'm actually not into self-flagellation," he replied lightly,
and the crowd roared.

She zipped down the front of her uniform and bent over
towards him. "Ever see any like these up close and real?" she
asked lasciviously. The men peered over to get a look too, pushing each other roughly.

"I was breast fed, yes," the Lama answered sweetly.

She looked at him closely, detecting that he was human.
From the planet below. That made him all the more attractive
in her eyes. She yearned to rape, pillage and plunder the planet
below, and she could start right now with the raping part. This
strong-looking boy would be no match for her strength, for she
was of the Rakshasa species, which had far greater physical
strength than humans.

What is he doing on the ship? We must have brought him up? One-way trip for him then— whatever I do to him is better than what's left in store for him. She moved in closer to have her way with him.

The Lama knew what she had in mind and thought fast. An inspiration came to him, which would require his later apology to the woman. Maybe he could talk his way out of it, though, and not have to play this dirty trick.

"What's your name, Mommy?" he asked, pretending that she was like a mother to him. She stopped moving toward him, offended.

"I'm not old enough to be your mother, you little jerk-off." Her manner then turned briefly alluring. "You know they call me Glitu," she said.

He looked at her in neutral, reading in her mind what she was about to say.

"It stands for Greatest Lay In The Universe," she said proudly. Now she had gotten herself really hot and reached for the Lama.

She had him down on the ground and stripped and started to ride him. Except it wasn't him. The Lama stood with the astonished crowd staring at Glitu raping a bonobo—except that the creature was all in favor of it, so it wasn't actually rape. This was the Lama's dirty trick. If he had had more time, he could have been gentler perhaps. He would make it up to her at some point in the future, when the opportunity presented.

The black-suited sailors cheered on Glitu and the bonobo, and soon other bonobos joined in the frolic. The red-suited soldiers were mortified and tried to peel her off but were overpowered by the sailors there in greater number for the moment. More red-suits headed over as news spread telepathically to everyone in the ship.

As the fight turned nasty and guns came out, the Lama withdrew back up the ramp, turned a corner, and disappeared. *Nothing more I can do here, just let it play out,* he told himself.

17

Guess he had to leave in a hurry, no love note, Cholmondeley thought, balefully regarding the crumpled five-dollar bill left by the bedside by Ari or whoever that was. *Ari never gave me cash. That couldn't have been Ari. Ari had more class.*

He felt relieved and happy that his pimping days were over. It had only been three days and now he was well rid of the whole affair. He headed for his favorite scotch, and thus fortified, called to report that Ari had gone missing.

Perse was annoyed at having to cut short his sex bingeing. Reappearing on the ship, he found the battle in the park had turned into a civil war between his two armed services. He had always encouraged friction between them and would normally just sit down and watch the fun, but he didn't like having to be summoned.

"At ease!" he bellowed, and the shooting stopped. "War's over, kids, get back to work. All leave suspended."

The troops moaned at this.

"Your own fault!" he roared and the moaning turned to whimpering. *That's better,* he thought.

He considered returning to Earth to resume playing Ari the space stud but now that seemed anticlimactic. *Never go back, always forward.*

So instead, he went to visit the Danang Lama, bringing the promised contract. It was over 900 pages of small print, as his contracts always were. He anticipated a great deal of fun, only to find to his great dismay that the Lama had somehow escaped. Now he was mad, really mad.

"Search the ship!" he yelled, motioning for this to be broadcast everywhere.

Everyone on board heard him yelling it in their minds anyway, leaving a faint trace of headache in its wake. Supervisors led subordinates in each sector of the ship but as the hours went on and the ultra-sophisticated equipment failed to find the Lama, Perse sat down astonished.

"He has to be on the ship!" he said to himself aloud in supreme consternation. "No shuttles are missing, there's no other way a human could get back down to the planet!"

Ω

The real Ari obeyed the orders of his dominatrix Kaitanya, while Nastassia watched in fascination. The three of them had been locked in a single suite of a sprawling Long Island estate by their captors, whom they now knew to not be the police.

The sex activity surprised Ari and Nastassia because for the first day Kaitanya would not even speak to either of them. The real Kaitanya, fully aware of everything that was happening, couldn't tell Ari and Nastassia that she was under the control of a being on the side of their captors—she had no control over anything, Goma was in complete control. And Goma, bored to distraction by the second day, came up with this sex activity as the only thing she could think of to break the boredom. *Maybe I'll get bored again and have to rape the girl.*

This sudden behavior by her fellow prisoners got Nastassia feeling very sexually aroused. She found that she liked the feeling, and felt it was an okay way to feel even without doing anything to relieve the tension. And it felt better than endless and pointless conversations with Ari while Goma-as-Kaitanya pretended to not hear. They had no way to get out, and she prayed for intervention as the only course of action left to her, continuing to pray while watching the sadomasochistic sex games.

Some of their captors must have been watching because the door opened just as the sex games ended. In walked Otto with three skinheads of various nationalities, all brandishing firepower. Ari and Goma-as-Kaitanya began to put some of their clothes back on, and Ari started speaking while pulling his pants up.

"Otto, I'm so glad to see you," he said.

Otto smiled menacingly. "Sit down, my friends. I intend to enlighten you," he taunted, his gun pointing directly at Ari.

The three prisoners sat down on the floor, their backs against the bed rails. Goma-as-Kaitanya pulled down the bedding to cushion her back. Otto sat facing them, with the thugs standing all around. He seemed excited by this opportunity to say the things he was about to say.

"Our organization has existed on Earth since the 1930s, when it was founded by the Armanen—you know them as The Leaders. They were the first gods on this planet," Otto professed. "In June 1945 many of the richest of us were able to evade Nuremberg. Our leader was widely believed to be dead, and we laid low for a few years until we were able to meet again in Madrid. We had met near Munich in *April* of 1945, knowing we were about to lose the war, to create the plan we've been carrying out ever since—our plan to come back to power."

"Nazis..." Ari blurted, aghast to learn this wasn't just about Hitler, that the Nazis had been operating invisibly for over half a century.

"Labels... belief systems..." Otto said in a fatherly tone. "Try to listen with your whole mind, without preconceptions, Ari—get high or die."

Otto swept his arms upward to address the whole room and seemingly beyond. "As Ari has seen, *der Führer* is alive, and is the Leader of the Armanen!" he boomed threateningly. "He is much more than a human being."

He looked around, meeting the eyes of his audience, and saw not a trace of doubt.

Ari froze. He saw a brief vision of monochrome newsreel footage of giant rallies and fist-pounding speeches and gas chambers and ovens. Chills ran up and down his spine.

"The plan requires complete demoralization, disintegration of existing governments and economic systems—a vacuum in which *der Führer* will be drafted on a white horse," Otto patiently explained.

"Remember the two Kennedys that got shot?" Otto asked suddenly, and they tried to remember their "ancient" history. Their eyes widened as they remembered.

Ari had heard some of this before from Otto.

"Marilyn Monroe? The Pope—we missed on that one. And we only wounded Reagan." Otto looked proud nonetheless, his smile sinister. "Nine-eleven?"

Ari recalled that one vividly and stared in shock and awe.

"If it was impeccably planned and executed, that's a sign *we* did it," Otto went on. "Have you noticed a gradual deterioration of the people willing to be visible leaders? The increase of militant groups from terrorists to gangs to rogue nations? The rise of new diseases? Hate dominating social media? The house of cards economy? The ubiquitous larceny? Spurring on of bad debt? Political parties going to all-out war with each other? Politicians acting in ultra-radical ways? Schools turned into shooting galleries?" His chest swelled. "Have we brilliant minds or not? Has not destiny chosen us to ultimately, inevitably rule?"

"You have certainly made great strides in controlling the course of history on this planet," Goma-as-Kaitanya cooed, intending to sound to Ari and Nastassia like a gallant adversary in awe.

Ari was still in shock and Nastassia sat poker-faced, thinking fast. Nastassia knew all about World War Two and Hitler, she had been an avid reader on those subjects before she was ten. For Hitler to still be alive with his organization still having impact on a global level, the world was in even worse trouble than she had ever imagined. As she listened to Otto, she had automatically shielded herself against how she felt about

all this, using her time and energy most efficiently to deter-
mine her course of action. She directed her attention to take
in everything.

"Thank you, my dear," Otto acknowledged. "And now for
your roles."

Suddenly riveted, the three captives gave Otto their undi-
vided attention.

"Ari," Otto began, "you know your place now. I expect when
I say 'heel' you will not hesitate. You are in for a lot more love-
making as we propagate connections with The Leaders. I will
expect a lot more expressions of gratitude from you—and no
complaints—otherwise, you know, we also need male agents
connected with The Leaders."

Hearing this, the thugs, all now obviously gay, leered at Ari
and he shivered involuntarily.

"I'll be good," Ari said meekly. "Sorry if I've ever been rude
or ungrateful, Otto. I'll make it up to you." Secretly, he har-
bored deep hopes of escaping this fate somehow. *Even death
might be better,* he told himself.

"Kaitanya and Nastassia, we intend to sell you back to the
Russians, or to the highest bidder," Otto announced. Then,
looking coy, he cocked his head and smiled. "Under certain
circumstances we might just *give* you back to the Russians."

Both women smiled, but Nastassia had feigned hers. She
saw only a faint pinprick of light at the end of this dark tunnel
of her present life. She put all her faith in it.

That evening Hitler visited Otto in his bedroom and gave
him new orders, without any explanation, leaving Otto stu-
pefied. In the middle of the night the guards rushed in and
grabbed Goma-as-Kaitanya, dragging her off while some piled
on Nastassia and Ari to keep them from interfering. The guards
then left the two behind locked doors and could be heard join-
ing the other guards as they manhandled Goma-as-Kaitanya
away.

When they could hear nothing any more, Ari and Nastassia
looked at each other, wondering if that was going to happen to

each of them, and what would happen when they were dragged off? Torture? Sleep did not come easy for the rest of that night.

Ω

Behemoth hung silent, very high up in the moonless black night sky over Long Island. The estate below and its stately lawns looked very close through the cameras. They could see people through the bay windows. They caught glimpses of Ari and Nastassia walking about freely in one suite. For some reason the other Russian woman didn't come near the windows, or maybe she was being kept someplace else.

"Six guards in the big house with Otto plus an older servant woman," Donna reported.

The agents stood in the main bridge on the underside of Behemoth surrounded by night through the armored glass windows. Captain Miller listened in from his post at the controls.

"There are some number of armed fighters in the small building," Seana added.

"Two sentries out in the bush to the north," Khan put in.

"Another two, one east and one west, just off the beach in the scrub," Page reported.

"They could be planning to take them out by sub," Shannon speculated. "We have to hit them before they make it to the sub. We might need to bring in the Navy and Coast Guard," he mused aloud.

"I have a feeling we might make things worse by trying for a rescue," Williams countered. "Can we try for mind contact with Ari and Nastassia?"

Everyone thought that sounded like a good idea. They fell silent as each one tried to make contact.

Minutes went by. Then Seana said, "Ari is despondent and hoping either for rescue or death. Apparently they have him caught up in some desperate situation where he would rather die than go through whatever it is. I'm not sure he knows I was in his mind trying to make contact."

Khan nodded in agreement. He had picked up something like that, just not so clear.

"Nastassia knew it was me," Jason said, almost boasting. "She asked us not to create a violent conflict. She thinks it's going to work itself out some other way."

The others looked dubious, unsure of the Russian agent's trustworthiness to them. Maybe she had joined their side, maybe not.

"I got that from her too," Seana said.

"They are hoping to sell the Russian agents back to the Russians," Williams relayed. "Or to the highest bidder. Or maybe they'll use them as a bargaining chip to get something else they want even more than money from the Russians."

"We had better wait," Shannon concluded. "But be ready for action, if we detect a sub. Donna, please contact the Navy and Coast Guard and put them in the picture."

Donna went to the comms station and lit it up.

Ω

Templegard lay in a cornfield peering through binoculars at the terrorist encampment below not far from Vahnabad, Iran. He wished he knew why these particular terrorists were so important. He didn't even know what they called themselves. His handlers referred to them simply as the Blueturbans. They all wore blue turbans. He had even seen their leader a couple of times from close up—half the time he also wore a blue turban, in his case apparently only for certain formal occasions. He had fierce eyes, a booming and frightening voice that sounded unearthly, and a long dark beard. He looked about forty and in good shape.

Templegard had hung upside down in that dank Turkish prison for days, being alternately beaten, interrogated, and fed. He knew that he would reach a point where his strength would be insufficient to escape, should an opening arise, so he had to make his move before that point, even if the opening wasn't ideal. But he couldn't let himself be rushed into moving at the wrong time. Moment to moment his intuition worked on the timing optimization problem. In between, his dream lover would contact him and his strength would be built up again. He pretended to his captors, the Blueturbans, to be weaker than he really was.

He had escaped, been resupplied, taken a day off to recover a bit, but never let the Blueturbans out of his sight. They had moved out of Turkey and into Iran. They seemed to be heading to Teheran but were encamped southwest of that city.

Down in the valley the Blueturbans had set up their camouflaged camp, in the center of which stood a large tent covered with shrubbery to conceal it from the air, as with the rest of the smaller tents circled around it. In the larger tent the human body of Perse sat at a field desk looking at a large monitor. He was on a Zoom call with Russian Field Marshall Berla.

"I understand you know where my daughters are," Berla said over the nonsecure connection.

"Yes, they are under my protection in the U.S.," Perse responded. "As a gesture of friendship I have already released one of them and she is on her way to you now. I'm eager to return the other one safely to you, but I have a little favor to ask on a more secure connection, which we can set up."

Berla realized he needed to bring his superiors into this, or he himself would be at great risk. He agreed nonetheless. "Yes, by all means let's set up a secure connection."

Ω

Berla stood at attention in front of the Russian president's desk.

"At ease, Field Marshall, please sit down and pour," the Russian president said. Berla dutifully sat and poured the iced vodka into their glasses. "*Za zdarovye*," they intoned in unison, clinking glasses, then sipping.

"How is our agent—Colonel Astrolova?" the president asked.

"She seems fine," Berla responded. "Whatever softness she had before is gone, but that's to be expected, after space travel, sex with an alien, and being kidnapped by terrorists. It's her strong recommendation that we work with Perse's terrorists. She is psychically sure that they are mercenaries hired by the aliens."

Berla didn't mention that Kaitanya had seduced him into becoming his mistress upon her return, right after he interrogated her, which he found unusual but not unwelcome. He didn't know that one of the aliens inhabited her and was waiting for the right moment to transfer her affections to the Russian president.

Kaitanya knew she could have gone insane, being trapped inside herself without control over anything. So instead, determined to find a way to extricate herself and get back in control of her body, she began to study her own intelligence as if it were an artificial intelligence, observing as closely as possible what Goma was doing inside the same mind. She found that Goma was installed in the left prefrontal and left temporal cortex. Kaitanya knew that's where language is processed and so she stopped using words and started thinking only in images and feelings, hoping to take over in the right cortex, and from there in the motor control center at the top of the head.

"What do you think he wants?" the president asked.

"He's not far from Teheran. We surmise that he wants our permission for him to take over Iran," Berla responded.

The president laughed. "A two-bit terrorist is going to take over Iran," he said ironically then grinned. *Berla must be pulling my leg.*

Berla nodded a little too vigorously, nervous in front of the president. "We think he may have kidnapped our agents to demonstrate to us that he is a force to be reckoned with."

"That's not like taking over Iran," the President said drily, wondering what he was missing.

Berla was quick to supply it. "Sir, Kaitanya—Colonel Astrolova—Psychotronic Division One believes that this Perse character is connected with the transmission, that there is a First Contact situation taking place, with Perse somehow working with these psychic extraterrestrials in a ship hovering invisibly over the Earth. Either that or someone has taken over many minds to cause them all to suffer the same mass hallucinations. That seems even less likely, sir."

Having said this out loud—and no less to the president— Berla suddenly realized how zany it all sounded and that he had now really sunk himself.

The president paused before reacting. "Field Marshall, thanks for your courage in speaking that out loud. GRU has been beating around that same bush but afraid to put it out there in so many words."

"Whew," Berla said involuntarily, feeling saved. Now that it was on the table, both men sat back contemplating the enormity of it. Aliens contacting humans for the first time. The stuff of movies but now actually *happening*.

To the president's way of thinking, Russia could not ignore the opportunity to lead the rest of the world in becoming friendly with this power, whether *its* intentions were friendly or not.

And furthermore, if the aliens' agent or ally, Perse, with their help could actually take over Russia's biggest client state, they had better get friendly with him too. And then get to meet the aliens and make the best deal possible. Before anyone else.

18

The Nazis had kidnapped three people without checking with Perse. They had a submarine on its way to the U.S. that they had not told Perse about either. Although he was their *Führer*, they had a penchant for making their own decisions. They could never forget how he had ultimately made the wrong decisions last time, almost a century ago.

When the Coast Guard reported to Theta that they had spotted a sub nearing the Long Island estate, Shannon's hand was forced. They could not sit idly by and let an American citizen and two Russian agents slip out of their grasp and into the hands of an unknown foe.

"We go now," Shannon said.

"Otto is going to use his three hostages to force us to stop shooting," Williams predicted.

Shannon nodded grudgingly. "Makes no difference."

"If we have to be taken prisoner to save their lives, that's what we should do, and then figure out how to take back the situation from there," Williams said hurriedly as they put on communicator helmets and body armor and weaponized themselves.

On their backs they brought armor and weapons for the three hostages. Each psychic Theta soldier had been trained to independently target and fire two small arms at the same time, one in each hand, by partitioning their minds. Williams recalled that individuals who had played the piano had been easier to train. In simulated combat situations this mind partitioning had been shown to work. It had never been tested in actual combat until now. The troops carried the FN SCAR, a small machinegun almost as reliable as the AK-47 but far more precise and customizable. The bullet tips were hardened for armor piercing.

"Copy that," Shannon said.

He nodded to Captain Miller, who started a rapid silent descent.

"Release the predators," Shannon said.

Miller tapped on his console. From underneath Behemoth came four predator drones. They flew off noisily into the night and then all was quiet again.

Shannon looked at the second hand on his watch. "Now," he said simply.

Miller tapped and sent the code. Two miles out to sea a destroyer launched a cruise missile.

Behemoth descended more slowly and the Theta agents stepped over to their jump stations and grabbed their respective rappelling lines.

"Okay," Shannon yelled, and Miller opened the bay and the six of them fell out of Behemoth, slowing their descent using the lines, until they touched down atop the main house of the estate.

Suddenly the night lit up with an awful clamor as the smaller adjoining building blew up with whatever troops had been in there. More or less simultaneously the sentries were killed by the predators. The Theta agents made their way into the main building by smashing their way in through windows.

Williams had climbed through an attic window and found himself in total darkness. He figured that the second house where the troops had been garrisoned was also the generator power center that fed electricity into the main house. The cruise missile had taken out the extra troops and also, he now assumed, the lights in the main house.

He moved soundlessly through the dark, seeing everything in green through his infrared goggles. No one else was there. He sensed his comrades wherever they were progressing in a similar manner of total stealth. The sounds arising since Behemoth descended were beneath human autonomic trigger level, with the exception of the smashing glass sound on their entry. Somewhere ahead were mercs with weapons at the ready. Only ten seconds had passed but the defenders were already soundless themselves. Williams felt a satisfied feeling to be up against professionals. He moved without pause to the dropdown stairs. Until he heard the gunshots.

Shannon too was in total darkness in an unoccupied guest room. It smelled like it had not been used in a while although there was nothing offensive in that smell. He moved without hesitation toward the one door. Until he heard the gunshots.

Seana had come in on the captives and motioned silence as they woke up fast. She went to the door and listened. Hearing nothing and her extra senses allowing it, she flung open the door and dove left, her weapon ready. Seeing no one in the corridor she rolled left, making minimal sound. The two captives had come out and she rose and led them through a corridor toward the north—she knew from their research that this corridor became a mezzanine. She made sure to stay ahead of them as they were unarmed. She could see well enough in the total darkness with her infrared goggles. Then she heard the gunshots.

Donna found herself in a bedroom where the occupant of the bed was an older Hispanic woman. She administered a sedative in the neck and the woman went back to sleep without saying a word. Donna then went to the door and listened, hearing gunshots, far louder than she expected.

Khan and Jason crashed through onto the main floor and directly into a firefight. Their adversaries had the same infrared gear and could see them just as well. The two martial artists fired as they rolled across the floor in a dicey maneuver, finding luck on their side as they took out the two shooters. They quickly checked out the rest of the room, found it empty, and with fast hand gestures went out in opposite directions through two of the three exits from the main sitting room.

Seana, followed by Nastassia and Ari—who had hurriedly donned the armor Seana provided and now also had a gun in hand—emerged onto the balconied mezzanine looking down at the main sitting room below with the two merc corpses. Nastassia telepathed to Seana that Kaitanya had been gone for days and had probably been returned to Russia, so Seana abandoned the armor brought for Kaitanya and the two women instantly jumped over the railing, landing surprisingly softly. They took the weapons and ammo from the corpses. A moment later, Ari landed, softly in his case by landing on the largest couch. He found the dead mercs also had sidearms and knives, which he nicked.

From the next room to the left they heard more gunshots. Nastassia got to the door first, diving into the room and rolling while her mental senses looked for signs of life. Gunshots revealed a shooter and she shot him. His death scream might scar her forever, she thought, then instantly put it aside.

Someone else shot at her from two o'clock, missing her, and as she swung her gun in that direction, Seana killed the shooter.

A dark quiet settled in the room. Seana sensed the two captives breathing silently. *I have the two captives, third not here,* she telepathed, hoping the other Theta agents would get her message.

Back to the roof with them now, Shannon replied telepathically. He tapped a button on his phone to let Captain Miller know it was time to extricate them. Williams, Khan and Jason also heard this and headed back up to the roof, revealing a degree of psychic efficacy that had never been demonstrated before within Theta. The transmission had apparently given them a permanent power boost.

Suddenly a bullet hit Seana in the shoulder. She spun around. The bullet had been stopped by the armor but had possibly broken something anyway. At least three or four mercs stood at the doorways into the main sitting room, shooting at them, and they all shot back except for Seana, who was catching her breath and checking her functionality, leaning against the wall.

Upstairs! Blimp coming, Seana telepathed. They got off the exposed balconied mezzanine and ran to the windows they had smashed their way in through. Getting back up on the roof was not so easy—the ropes they had come down on were gone—but they all somehow scrambled and climbed their way up to the roof. Seana, with one side of her body mostly out of action, had the hardest time but made it. The seven of them—five rescuers and two freed captives—crouched with weapons pointed at the threat vectors in all directions while stealing glances upward in eager anticipation of seeing Behemoth block out the stars in its soundless descent. But where was it?

Suddenly a fusillade of shots rang out and they all instinctively ducked but had no cover. Some of the mercs, realizing that attacking through the windows would have been a bad tactic, had gone outside and found arboreal sniper positions covering the roof. The Theta agents and their liberates returned fire at the muzzle flashes in the trees. Finally a big black slow-moving mass blocking out the stars drew closer.

Gunfire from the trees and ground now escalated suddenly from all directions. Apparently there were many more defenders than had been detected through recons. The Theta agents and their cohorts had been efficiently taking out the owner of any muzzle flash that appeared, but now it appeared impossible to not be killed by the relentlessly withering fire.

From Nastassia's point of view, time stopped. She knew she was in someone's crosshairs. If she moved to escape, time would resume and she would die. She somehow felt this as a certainty, as if God was talking to her.

It was God in a larger sense, but specifically it was Templegard. In his dream he was hovering over the house. His dream woman was down there with the rest of his buddies and they were all in dire trouble. It was up to him to do something, but what? His dream body seemed to have no arms or legs to do anything with.

Nastassia kept trying to figure out what to do without moving. She sent her mind out to find the shooter who was targeting her, and there he was. His name was Boris Embler. He was not a Nazi. He was a GRU Spetsnaz superspy who had infiltrated the Nazis. In this eternal space outside of time she learned everything about him.

As a child of a military father, he had been encouraged to study the history of war and espionage. When he read about the exploits of Richard Sorge, the top Russian superspy of World War Two, he became inspired by this role model. At about the same time he became enamored of the James Bond films, and he shaped himself to be a blend of his two heroes. He was somewhat older than the Nazis he now fought alongside with, and of higher rank, but he managed to get away with being simply a soldier of fortune drawn to the shared fascist ideals.

The order from Berla to kill Nastassia if she appeared to have joined forces with the Americans placed this Spetsnaz superspy here now, his finger half clenched on the trigger. His fifty-caliber sniper rifle with its large flash suppressor was specially designed to pierce the best American body armor. The bullet, with its titanium jacketed tip fashioned after the shaped charge of the American bazooka, contained a small explosive charge whose force would be channeled forward.

But I haven't joined the Americans, she telepathed to him. *They are rescuing us and I will be free to continue my mission for Psycho. By destroying me unnecessarily you will mortally wound our country's psychic lead.*

If he heard, she had no sign of it. He had been told to use his judgment and if in doubt, kill. That was not exactly Berla's intent, but as the orders came down the chain of command they had been unintentionally subtly modified in that direction. Boris was a consummate professional, a fearless coldblooded killer. That's what he wanted to become and he had achieved his life's goal. He was used to targets coming up with compelling reasons not to be killed and he ignored them as he now ignored Nastassia, if he heard her at all, his psychic abilities being as dormant as in most humans most of the time.

You know what you have to do, Templegard telepathed to Jason.

Not knowing if that thought came from the outside or from his own mind, Jason suddenly did know what he had to do.

I'll be seeing you, Jason telepathed to Nastassia as he flew forward in front of her, taking the bullets and going down.

Nastassia cried out and grabbed Jason before his body slid off the roof, tears streaming down her face.

Williams couldn't see the muzzle flash because of the suppressor but he sensed Boris Embler and fired a barrage of shots directly at him. Boris took a bullet across his right cheek as he slid rapidly backward down into cover, and the others on the roof fired at the spot in the trees still shaking under the pounding from Williams' carbine.

Behemoth ropes off to the north suddenly swooped in toward them, there to be grabbed just in time. But Williams waved Behemoth off, yelling into his throat mike to the Captain, "Get out of here! They have SAMs!" He had just picked up on several groups in the woods readying surface-to-air missiles capable of quickly dispatching Behemoth.

"Back in the house!" Shannon yelled. They scrambled back through the windows, narrowly escaping falls, the maneuver made more perilous with Seana wounded and Nastassia carrying Jason's lifeless body. They cleared each floor going down to the basement and covered all the directions outside.

Williams picked up on phosphorus rifle grenades being readied and a small mortar being set up. The house being all wood would go up like a torch if the mortar didn't kill them all first. He saw no way to get them out of the house alive.

"Incoming!" Williams yelled and they all hit the floor a moment before the first mortar shell took off the east wing of the house. *Bad shot,* Williams thought. *The next one will be right on top of us.* He put out a call for cosmic fire support. He had never done that before in his life. As an agnostic he had never seen a reason to do so. Now that he sensed in every second that he was connected to everything else, it suddenly seemed natural.

Surprising them all, another unforeseeable force entered from the west and the Nazis quickly turned away from them to deal with that foe.

"Rangers!" Seana yelled with joy, picking up on them psychically.

The agents, not under fire for the moment and seeing the action outside, were eager to support the U.S. Army Rangers in any way they could. The friendlies had pushed the Nazis back to the east and suddenly everything was lit up as if by daylight. A flare or some other device had been set off, making the two groups now in hand-to-hand combat totally visible. More distant shooters tried to pick off enemies without hitting friendlies.

Seemingly out of nowhere, a teenage boy appearing to have no fear sauntered toward the combatants. The shooting stopped. Everyone in the area appeared transfixed, captivated by this surreal interruption—somehow it just felt wrong to be pulling a trigger.

The Lama came up to the nearest Nazi, looked at his automatic rifle, and asked in a friendly, loving way, "Can I see that please?"

Inexplicably the skinhead simply handed the rifle over to him. Then, in perfect monkey drill, the Lama twirled the weapon, sensing its balance points perfectly at once, and ended in a Queen Anne Salute.

As he handed the rifle back to the man, he looked around at everyone with love emanating from every part of his being. A couple of the tough-looking men sighed. Then something overwhelming happened. All of them slipped into the world Williams had entered. They realized their connection with everything around them. But they had accessed an even higher place than Williams. Looking out they each *knew* that "I am the One Self of the multiverse, playing all the other roles too".

The Nazi whose rifle the Lama had played with now looked at the Ranger he had been about to kill and saw that Ranger as himself. All around the lawn of the estate, men who had been about to kill each other instead hugged each other and cried tears of joy.

Williams asked himself, *Am I imagining this?*

19

"Jason," Khan cried to his student, hugging the body and getting blood all over himself. "You did the right thing, buddy," he choked, and put his head on Jason's like a father would. "Your father and your whole family are going to be so proud of you," he whispered in Jason's inert ear.

Jason's soul heard.

I'll be seeing you, Nastassia telepathed to Jason's soul. She sent him gratitude and respect, wanting him to know that he had redeemed himself of everything he hated himself for. *You are now free to succeed.*

I'm sorry I thought you arrogant, Seana pathed to Jason, tears welling in her eyes. "He was the one who came up with the idea of the challenge fight," she said aloud, and the others nodded. "Without that scenario, we might never have uncovered the Nazis in time."

Let's hope it's in time, she thought.

I lost a man, Shannon thought unhappily. *I hate when I do that.*

You're the best, Tim, he heard Jason's voice in his mind. Not having been a believer in life after death, Shannon slowly absorbed the shock.

Jase, now you're in a place where you can realize that all your life you tortured yourself, Williams pathed. *No one else was doing that to you. Remember that from now on. Bring*

186

that awareness into your next life, all your next lives. You never have to torture yourself again.

Thanks, Marty, Williams heard in his mind a moment or two later, after Jason's soul had assimilated his message.

Ari looked at the corpse with respect and measured himself against Jason. He found himself sorely lacking in many respects. He formed a vow to become as admirable a person as he now saw Jason to have been.

Ω

The group made it down the Behemoth's ropes to Ari's roof terrace. The huge dirigible moved swiftly and noiselessly off into the night.

U.S. agents met them there and took possession of Jason's body.

Ari slipped a vodka tonic into Nastassia's hand and clinked glasses, bringing her attention back into Ari's living room and its vast Manhattan panoramas.

"Navy got the sub to surface and surrender," Shannon reported, removing his cellphone from his ear. He put it down and accepted the single malt from Cholmondeley. The butler had sensed that his boss was back to normal, which made him happy.

Shannon toasted the team. "Sharp!" he said. Their first performance as a combat team exceeded his wildest expectations. "You too!" he raised his glass to Nastassia, and then Ari. They had both performed like pros. He looked at Nastassia—suddenly realizing how young she was. *There's something familiar about her...*

"I'm very grateful to you all for saving us," Nastassia said genuinely. "You too, Ari," she added affectionately. "Thank you, all. Will I be able to go home now—assuming those are my orders—" she mused aloud.

"Of course," Shannon said. "You and the company of GRU Spetsnaz in Manhattan have spent good tourist dollars doing the usual things, and committed no crimes."

This was the party line he had been given. New York's Sullivan Act gun law had been shattered to bits but the U.S. government preferred to ignore that infraction for diplomatic reasons. Détente with all other countries had been the foundation of Gomez's election campaign. With hate and violence having become ever-present in almost all communities around the world, the preacher of peace could now be heard.

The president also had new reasons to want the Russians as friends. Beings from space had made their presence known and they might be more dangerous than any other humans, so it was high time to band the human race together—while also extending a welcome to the extraterrestrials, who for some reason had not yet made contact. *Had they made contact with other nations?* Gomez wondered.

"Hitler is alive," Ari said somberly. "I've seen him. He's not a human being. He's the ruler of the aliens. He's definitely a threat to the human race, not a friend."

"The Nazis went underground in 1945 and have been carrying out a plan of world destabilization ever since," Nastassia reported.

"So then, this Hitler of yours is an alien?" Williams asked. He suspected the answer to be somewhat more complicated, that maleficent aliens had been helping the Nazis back in World War Two as well as their extremist heirs, and that the human Hitler may have been inhabited and controlled by one of these aliens.

"Why did they give Kaitanya back to the Russians?" Ari asked.

She probably has one of them in her head, Williams thought, though it would be unwise to voice these sorts of ideas to the Russians. *Like the women who connected with The Leaders through Ari. She probably has a mission to psychically take over the Russian leadership.* He knew he would have to report this possibility up the chain of command so that the president could decide what to do about it, if anything.

"Oh my God," Shannon said. "Have to report all that." He stood and walked out, taking out his cell.

"Excuse me," Williams said, standing and following Shannon out.

In Ari's empty office Williams confided his thoughts about Kaitanya so Shannon could include that in his report to the President. Then he went back and rejoined the others.

Ω

"How did it go?" President Gomez asked.

Leaning his elbows on Ari's desk, his cell on speaker a few inches away, volume set low, Shannon said, "I lost a man, sir," not sounding as impassive as he had intended. His first priority was always to get his people out. His second priority was to get the mission done. He was beating himself up.

"Which one," Gomez asked sympathetically. *Not Williams, I hope.*

"Page, sir."

"Oh. Sorry. Good kid. I'll send a condolence to the family, of course." Gomez, at his desk in the Oval Office, nodded to his assistant.

"He took a bullet to protect the Russian agent, sir," Shannon reported, implying posthumous medals and some potential political capital.

"That's a very interesting angle, Tim," the president said, thinking of the upcoming election. "Tim, when you get a chance, please email me with some thoughts about Page's — what was his first name?"

"Jason, sir."

"—Jason Page's finest qualities—what a great American he was," Gomez concluded. "What was his ethnic background?" he asked as an afterthought. His mind was spinning rapidly.

"African American, sir."

Good! Gomez thought.

"Sir, there's much more I have to tell you," Shannon said, sensing the president was about to end the call. *Did I pick that up psychically,* he wondered.

"Yes?"

"Sir, Ari Mann says that Hitler is alive and he has seen him—he is nine feet tall and the head of an alien invasion whose last big push was as the Nazis," Shannon said, suddenly feeling ridiculous.

Gomez in fact laughed softly and very briefly. "I know how you feel saying that to me but we know it already. That's why I sicced you on Ari," he revealed, pausing before he added, "although I haven't totally bought into all of it." Gomez instinctively spoke in a lower voice. He knew psychic powers are real and always felt some concern about possible psychic attacks on himself, so he acted as if the possibility that his mind was being read continuously, twenty-four-seven, was very real.

"Which part sir?" Shannon had the temerity to ask.

"Hitler—aliens—" Gomez began. "If I were head of the defeated Nazis who managed to escape, I would find it very useful to be able to claim backing by a superior alien race."

"Obviously we're ready to do whatever you say, sir, but we should get under the hood of this thing real fast," Shannon said professionally, covering his disappointment that the top had no idea what was true. That meant Gomez might send Theta off on some wasteful course, giving this threat—whether terrestrial or otherwise—enormous advantage. He steeled himself to fight against any idea he felt did not go for the jugular.

Some minutes later Shannon came back to the gathering on Ari's terrace. "Otto's dead," he announced what the president had passed along. "Sudden heart attack."

"Cyanide pill in a tooth or something." Ari suspected this would be Otto's usual style.

"Something," Shannon agreed, "but not cyanide, he didn't turn blue. The president was amused to also inform us that Russia had complained about the treatment of their diplomat personnel—those Spetsnaz who thought they were surrendering to the New York City police when it was actually the Nazis."

"What happened to those guys anyway?" Khan asked.

"The Nazis took their weapons and released them, then got in their fake cop cars, turned on the bubble gum machines, and roared deafeningly away into the sunset."

Intent on returning to the business at hand, Williams asked, "Do we have orders?"

"Not yet. The president actually knew about all of this, said that's why he assigned us to Ari," Shannon confided cautiously, seeking to not go too far but wanting to be fair to everyone involved. "They're still trying to figure out our orders." *As usual,* he said to himself.

Ari had a question. He looked at Khan. "That story you told me... that you are the true leaders..." Ari began uncertainly, "that was just a story, right?"

They all looked at each other. Williams felt he had no right to speak before Shannon so held back. After a silent pause, they all looked to Shannon.

"I don't know, Ari," Shannon admitted. "Sometimes I feel like I've lived before and this... mission is a continuation..." He trailed off.

Seana looked at Williams who had still not fully shared his visions with Shannon.

Out of character, Shannon turned to Williams. "What do you think, Marty?"

Williams looked him in the eyes and made a faint eye gesture toward Ari.

"You may speak freely," Shannon said, exceeding his authority and knowing it. He felt sure that Ari was a loyal American who had a right to know whatever of a non-military nature Williams might have discovered. And he saw Nastassia as an enemy agent that he felt intuitively some bond with—what could she or the Russians do with information about whether some top American psychics felt they had worked together in previous lives? Use that to trick them? He didn't feel he could be manipulated in that way because he didn't particularly care whether it was true or not. It seemed irrelevant.

"I've seen portions of my earlier lives," Williams began quietly. "I've told Seana but held back from telling you, Tim, because I felt like there would be a right time."

They sat forward in rapt attention as he went on, carefully choosing his words.

"I don't know how many of us this affects," Williams continued, "but for sure you, me and Seana have worked together many times before."

Shannon, normally skeptical, took this in without resistance. "What's our mission?" he asked.

"I wish I knew," Williams responded earnestly.

Almost a minute passed in silence.

"I don't think this bears reporting up," Shannon concluded. "I mean, I think I believe it, but I don't know what would be gained by sharing it..."

They looked at Ari and Khan, who nodded they would keep the secret. Then they looked at Nastassia, who looked at Seana.

"I know that Seana and I have worked together in previous lives, and we were sisters in at least one of them," Nastassia confided. That left everyone speechless, although Seana nodded in agreement.

Nastassia looked at Williams. "You too," she said uncertainly. "You've been with us too. I think—" she hesitated and blushed slightly, "—I think you were my father at least once."

Williams stared at her, not knowing what to say, his instincts divided—conscious of the fact that she was an enemy agent, and a powerful one.

Cholmondeley came into the living room to announce a visitor was coming up.

Williams sensed danger and stood up. His manner caused them all to stand up and get ready for something.

Ari and the butler knew that people were not just sent up, the doorman or his backup would first call to see if the visitor was welcome.

"Did they give a name?" Ari asked, controlling his rising angst.

Cholmondeley's face turned red with chagrin. "Lucky Shickelgruber," he said. Everyone looked at each other to see if anyone recognized the odd name.

"It's Hitler," Williams said, and took out his gun.

The others followed his lead, except for the butler. *Let them think I'm unarmed,* the butler said to himself.

The elevator doors parted and in the darkness they could not make out a figure. Then Hitler stepped out smiling, dressed in a 1945 German Army Waffen SS uniform. He stood well under nine feet, at five feet nine inches.

Ari was terrified at seeing him again, even though this time in a shorter version. He covered his fear manfully.

"Adolf Hitler, I take it?" Williams asked, in a not unkind fashion.

"Martin Williams, I take it?" Hitler replied smugly and sauntered into the living room, taking off his black gloves, and then slapping them in his left palm every now and then. He sat down in the middle of the largest sofa, right between Nastassia and Seana. Everyone else sat cautiously, guns at the ready. Perse looked at the guns and smiled. He didn't want them to link this Hitler being with himself just yet. By pretending to be human, he could let them keep thinking that bullets could stop him.

"You've kept yourself so well," Seana kidded him. "You don't look 135 years old. Not a day over 134."

Hitler laughed indulgently and poured himself a single malt, toasted them, and sipped. "I have my secrets," he admitted. He had never been much of a drinker in his Hitler incarnation but the burning scotch felt good now.

"I've read about you," Seana said. "You were—are an occultist. A world-ranging student of the hidden—I understand you sent your agents to many places in the world to investigate occult records and in search of occult relics. I can see how you might have unearthed secrets of longevity."

"Are you thinking of being CEO of my beauty line?" Hitler taunted, crossing his leg.

"We thought you might have loftier goals in mind," Williams said to Hitler.

Ari found his voice and stepped up. This was his home after all, so he felt obliged to ask, though politely and with a steady voice, "Yes, what brings you here this time of night?"

"Recruiting, you might say," Hitler said. "I want to offer you all the benefits of being on my side."

"What are those benefits?" Khan asked, not because he cared what Hitler had to say, but just to hear his own voice in this surreal situation.

"Being on the winning side rather than the losing side of a brutal conflict is one of the obvious main benefits," Hitler said. "But there are so many benefits and I'm happy to describe them for you."

"Please do," Khan invited.

"Right now you're all relatively unconscious—you know nothing about your real identities—who you've been before," Hitler said. "I can tell you who you really are—and were."

"Are you the one who told Jason he was Jesus?" Williams asked.

Hitler laughed. "Yes, that was to trick him," he admitted. "But I would not be tricking you. We'd be on the same side. It would be to my advantage for you all to be fully enlightened."

"Can we start that enlightenment part before we decide?" Williams asked, playing along.

"Ha-ha," Hitler laughed. "Of course, sure. Here we go. You are all gods. We all are gods. There is no naturally top god. The top god gets to be top god in fair competition."

"And unfair competition?" Nastassia asked matter-of-factly though not pejoratively.

Hitler roared with laughter. "That too!" he said gaily.

"*The Message* said just the opposite—that we are each the same One Self inside," Williams pointed out.

"Sure it did," Hitler agreed. "That was propaganda warfare from the Backstabber, the guy who claims to be the self who is inside all of us."

"How can we tell who is right?" Shannon asked his own troops.

"Which feels right to your innermost self?" Williams advised.

Even normally-agnostic Shannon, usually up for philosophical debate, felt that nothing would be gained by discussing religion. And in any case, his team would not likely side with Hitler in rejecting the idea of a naturally-occurring top god.

"Besides enlightenment, what else are you offering as benefits?" Shannon asked.

To the others he actually seemed interested but they knew deep down inside that Shannon was merely a very convincing actor. *Or was he?*

"Money, power, sex, the usual things, whatever you want," Hitler replied, as if all that was inconsequential and obvious.

"I've got all that," Ari said.

"Right now, yes..." Hitler agreed.

"You know, I don't think we're interested," Ari said with finality, looking around. "Thanks for the visit, next time make an appointment please." And then he froze in place, unable to move.

"I think we'll hear no more from the discourteous one tonight, don't you think?" Hitler sneered, demonstrating his power.

The others could see that Ari couldn't move, as if paralyzed. His eyes conveyed panic.

"Take it easy, Ari," Nastassia murmured. She saw Hitler looking at her as if she was going to be the next one to be frozen in place and she felt a fear spike that she quickly controlled.

The spike propagated, however, and alerted Templegard as he slept in a horizontal bed-seat on an airplane, dreaming as usual. In his dream he was back with his buddies and his dream woman in an unmistakable Manhattan apartment.

Actually he was not so much with them as hovering over them. He knew they could not see him nor sense his presence in any other way. He saw them having a face-off with a dark messy-haired uniformed officer with a funny mustache. The situation seemed on the brink of violence.

"I don't mean to be impolite," Nastassia said, "but I need to get back to my people." She tried to stand up but couldn't— not frozen in place but denied that particular movement.

Templegard loosed his mightiest mindblast at the officer, who looked momentarily disconcerted, then held his head.

"A sudden headache," Hitler commented, and seemed to look around. His eyes lit on Templegard, invisible to the others. *Ah, Templegard,* he thought, strangely respectful of his ancient enemy, whom he had bested and puppeted but had never been able to entirely obliterate. Templegard now felt unable to move and could not send another mindblast. He paused to consider his options.

The elevator doors parted open again and everyone who could move turned and looked. Hitler then clamped down paralysis and unconsciousness on all of them. A figure stepped out—the Danang Lama.

"I can't believe I hadn't recognized you," Hitler said. "But when you got off the ship without a shuttle, I knew."

The Lama walked over and sat down amiably near Hitler.

"You're looking at me as if you have something to say," Hitler said.

"The One Self wants us to play closer to the Lost Lamb Rules," the Lama said.

"Why would I care what the Backstabber wants?" Hitler asked bitterly.

"I thought you'd want to know that He's going to do a Reset," the Lama said.

Hitler was shocked. "He's never done that before!"

The Lama nodded. "He likes to surprise himself. Don't you?"

"What's in it for me?" Hitler asked.

"One part you'll like is that knowledge of your possessed humans, like Kaitanya, will be forgotten by the Theta and Psycho agents, and by anyone to whom they have already reported these suspicions. Williams and the others won't remember having already put two and two together," the Lama divulged. "It's a penalty I earned by crossing the line, revealing the oneness to end the firefight when your Nazis were about to take out the Theta agents...."

"You're saying that just to get me to go along with it," Hitler said. "What am I not going to like about the Reset?"

"You may like all of it. My existence will be as if it had never occurred. No Danang Lama."

"Must say, I like that part too!" Hitler said, warming to the idea of the Reset.

"What else?" he asked, like a kid at Christmas, wondering what other toys they had for him. *What luck that bro screwed up,* he thought happily.

"No one will remember contact with spacecraft or aliens," the Lama said. "They won't remember seeing Hitler alive again either."

Perse didn't let it show but he was awed that the backstabber could even think of editing the minds of billions of Earthlings to forget the Danang Lama—what would they think of when they remembered the news stories about the big meeting at the UN? It boggled his mind, which made him angry. *That bastard must have conned or enslaved billions of software engineers—why don't I do that too?!*

The Danang Lama could of course read Perse's mind, and so, to assuage his concerns, said, "The One Self can easily do all that alone because S/He has infinite computing power. You cannot conceive that anyone has more power than you have, which is part of your hang-up."

Hitler thought about it for a moment, then yelled in rage, "So what's my leverage with the Russians then?! They're eager to cozy up to a superior alien race with space travel and super weapons!"

"You have made them cozy up to you already," the Lama said. "You've gotten their respect. They know you captured two of their best psychic agents and a powerful civilian psychic. They've got to realize that you must be a formidable psychic yourself."

"You think?!" Hitler interjected.

"Then there's Goma inside Kaitanya, about to be the most powerful woman in Russia," the Lama added.

Hitler nodded, admitting he was not really worried about losing the Russians. "Is there more?" he asked.

"No," the Lama said. "That's the deal, all of it."

For all his bravado, Perse knew he had no choice about the Reset but of course would never admit that aloud or telepathically. He relaxed and morphed into his Perse appearance. He checked out that his physical body back in Iran was safe. He'd be back in it and resume his strategy right after the Reset, which he figured must be imminent.

"Shall we?" the Lama said. He and Perse stood and walked to the elevator, rang for it, and boarded it when it came. When the elevator reached the lobby, its doors opened but no one was inside.

20

Ari stood and walked over to a large piece of classical statuary, the head of Homer on a marble capital. "This is the real thing," he said. "Otto and his people have enormous treasure troves of the most valuable art on Earth. Stolen from Jews, museums, everybody with private collections..."

"We have to find out the size of their organization. How big it was in 1945. How big it is now, almost ninety years later," Shannon mused. "With all that money..."

"I wonder how high up Otto was in the Nazi organization, and who the real leader is now," Ari thought aloud.

"We haven't gotten our orders yet," Shannon said guardedly in front of nonteam members. "I hope we get assigned to bring down the Nazis."

His comrades nodded agreement. Even Nastassia nodded.

"What are you going to do now?" Nastassia asked Ari.

He thought for a moment. "I've made enough money. I'm going to try to see if I can do some real good somehow."

She touched the back of his hand approvingly.

Khan stood up and said resolutely, "I'm going home to get some sleep." His teammates gathered around for a brief group hug and then he went down in the elevator, heading downtown to his apartment.

Williams rubbed Seana's shoulder gently where there was an angry red welt.

"Oh, that helps," she said tiredly.

He looked at her with love and went down on one knee. She noticed and laughed as if he was kidding.

"Seana, will you marry me?" he proposed.

"Ooohhh, of course, yes!" she said, flying into his arms.

Shannon hid his envy well and hugged them both, saying, "Congratulations, you two!"

"Mazel tov!" Ari said, hugging them.

"Good luck!" Nastassia said, hugging them.

For a brief moment they embraced in a group hug.

Something flitted through Williams' mind, and he had the sense of something in his mind being hidden from him, but he had no idea what it was.

To be continued in
PANDEMONIUM: Live to All Devices

It never ends...

ABOUT THE AUTHOR

Emmy® Award winner and media research industry leader, Bill Harvey has been lauded as a visionary of the changing mediascape over the last 35 years.

With an imaginative, unorthodox mind for research, innovation and invention, Bill started his career in the media business with a dream of making one-way media into something the audience co-creates. He predicted today's media reality with his *MediaWorld 1990* report to the industry, and in his widely-read *Media Science Newsletter*. He invented media research tools and measurement systems, including some now written into FCC regulations.

Bill became a leader in the field as media morphed into being more interactive, putting the viewer in charge. In 2022, Bill received an Emmy® Award for the pioneering development of technology which for the first time enabled privacy-protected measurement of the total audience of all cable/satellite-connected TV sets, and all Smart TV sets. In practical terms, this invention helps diverse audiences with a wide range of interests to get all the types of programs they enjoy the most.

Prior to receiving his Emmy® Award, Bill became the first recipient in 2014 of the Advertising Research Foundation's Erwin Ephron Demystification Award, and in 2008 he received the ARF's Great Mind Award. He holds four issued US patents and has consulted for over a hundred Fortune 500 companies.

Bill first experienced the Zone—that space where innovative and successful ideas and actions flow out of you effortlessly—as a young child. The son of legendary orchestra leader/emcee Ned Harvey and former Ziegfeld Follies showgirl Sandra Harvey, Bill started performing on stage at age four, dancing with showgirls and exchanging lines with comedic greats like Jack E. Leonard. He liked this feeling of being "on" and wanted to learn how to be "on" more often. So he began his lifelong quest to understand how to bring on higher states of consciousness and to help others do the same.

Earning his degree in philosophy, the first school subject he ever loved, Bill founded the Human Effectiveness Institute, with the goal of sharing the consciousness techniques he had learned and developed. His ideas were further inspired by Alan Watts, Buddhism, Zen, and by his adopted older brother, the multitalented Bill Heyer, second trumpet in Ned's band.

Bill's first book, **MIND MAGIC: The Science of Microcosmology**, met with rave reviews in the late 70s and was lauded by thousands of readers who returned the reader response cards inserted in the books—long before email and social media. Fans included John Lennon, Ram Dass, Norman Cousins, Daniel Goleman, and Jimmy Carter. The book is now available in its sixth edition, **MIND MAGIC: Doorways into Higher Consciousness** and continues to receive five-star reader reviews on Amazon.

In his second book, **YOU ARE THE UNIVERSE: Imagine That**, Bill speculates about the true nature of reality, in which all that exists is a single divine consciousness made of information. In this view, religion is not at odds with science.

Bill turned his theory into fiction, and conceived an epic series of novels entitled *Agents of Cosmic Intelligence*. **THE FIRST SON** was the first to be released, Episode 2 in the series, covering the ancient world and its great prophets—some of whom Bill sees as cosmically-inspired Agents.

PANDEMONIUM: Live to All Devices, Episodes 12 and 13 in the *Agents* series, is set quite a few years in our own future when new media technology has served up augmented reality and artificial people.

Bill lives with his wife Lalita and their cat Zohreh in the beautiful Hudson Valley. He has a daughter Nicole, and with Lalita has four grandchildren, Nicholas, Gabrielle, Jessica and Alexander. Jessica and her husband Andrew have now created Zara, giving Bill and Lalita their first great-grandchild.

AGENTS OF COSMIC INTELLIGENCE

the epic adventure chronicle of the universe

Imagine a world where everyone knows we are all One, together Whole.

The epic adventure series *Agents of Cosmic Intelligence* emerges from a unique viewpoint in which science and religion meld into a singular explanation that makes each person a vital part of the greatest real-life adventure in existence.

Agents of Cosmic Intelligence is a sweeping saga that unfolds forward and backward in time to become a story of the universe, how it might have "started" and where it might be "going."

BOOKS IN THE SERIES

THE GREAT BEING
Episode 1 | 200,000 BC—3068 BC   *Coming Soon*

There is a Great Rebellion going on throughout the Universe, all of which is a single Mind at play. Two Agents of Cosmic Intelligence, Melchizedek and Layla, are dispatched to infiltrate the Rebels on Earth. However, the Rebels have interfered with Earth evolution, so the human brains that the Agents step into repress their knowledge of who they really are.

THE FIRST SON
Episode 2 | 3067 BC—27 AD   *Published October 2018*

Rebel groups form nation-states to continue the endless wars they have propagated to make Earth people the toughest fighters in the Universe, to eventually storm the gates of Heaven and take over the Multiverse entirely. The First Son and the Agents quietly build up the character of Earth humans by incarnating as great Teachers, beginning and spreading that tradition across the planet.

PANDEMONIUM: Live to All Devices
Episodes 12&13 | Ca. 2035   *Published June 2022*

In this fast-moving thriller, a heady amalgam of hidden war, psychics, Nazis, aliens, artificial intelligence, virtual reality, and transcendental love takes place against a backdrop wherein the latest media/technology revolution triggers sudden unprecedented changes in world politics.

BOOKS BY BILL HARVEY

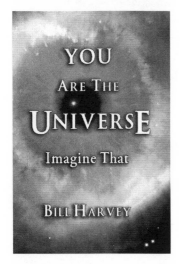

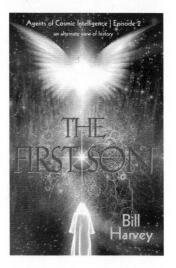

Available at your favorite bookstore and on Amazon.

BOOKS BY BILL HARVEY

MIND MAGIC
Doorways into Higher Consciousness

PANDEMONIUM
Live to All Devices

YOU ARE THE UNIVERSE
Imagine That

THE FIRST SON

THE MESSAGE